VEIL OF SHADOWS

ATHINA FERNWOOD

To those who have ever felt underestimated or out of place, may you find the strength within to reveal your true power. This story is for you.

Athina Fernwood

CHAPTER ONE

"A witch, a human, and a vampire walk into a bar."

My hands tightened around the glass in my hands. I have heard this joke too many times, and am not a big fan of the punch line. As a witch, you're not looked up to very much, more as a dog for the vampire creatures. Humans always say that there more useful because they need their blood making them safe, fucking blood bags.

The bar wasn't overly packed, mostly humans, there were maybe two vampires, then me, the witch. No one knew I was a witch, just a traveler looking for a drink. I had a particularly good skill set to keep my magic hidden. Humans could feel their skin tingle when we were close, vampires get nauseated. If a human brought in a witch to the Vampire Lord they would be rewarded greatly, if a Vampire found a witch, well if you didn't kill him you would find yourself wrapped up in chains before you could cast your first spell.

I sighed.

I could hear the group laughing. Shooting the rest of my drink I gave my thanks to the barman and left. This place was not a particularly good place to stay at, too many loyalists.

As I made my way down the road, I saw two vampires questioning people. They were looking for trouble or food, and if they drink from me, I'll be in trouble. It's not that they can't, it just hurts a lot...for them.

"You, stay there!" I didn't bother trying to play dumb and stopped where I was as they came towards me.

The one who spoke was older and had a scar over his right eye, definitely by a witch, that I bet was dead now. The other was young, naive, and who I'll have to focus my attention on to get out of this.

As they were coming to a stop in front of me, I bowed my head, "and what do I owe the pleasure to this visit?" I glanced up at the young one before straightening back up. A witch's glance could put anyone under a spell, even a vampire.

"We don't mean to bother..." The young one started but got smacked by the other, took a lot of control to not smile, I knew it worked.

"Don't play nice" he turned back to me "State your name and business."

"Angelic sir, I am here just passing through. I am staying at the inn just down the street." He had a curious look. Angelic is not a popular name but lying could put me in a worse position.

"What do you carry?"

"I have enough supplies for 3 days of food, and warm clothes for the fall air, sir."

He stepped in closer, "you sound like you're hiding something, don't bother lying to us, you know it's against the law."

"Sir I..."

"HELP! HELP!" we all turned towards where I had just come from. Someone was screaming coming out of the bar.

"Rig, we should go, she hasn't lied, and her business puts no one in danger."

"Careful Kai, you can never trust a traveler, but we will have to go." He turned towards me again, "I expect to find you later at the Inn."

"Of course." I bowed my head and they left. Assuming they would keep to their word I had no time to go back to the Inn. I needed to get out, fast.

Pacing myself quickly but not conspicuously quick. This town is just too close to Lord Gerard's palace, if he finds me, I would be put to trials in a heartbeat.

It was a dark night being almost to the new moon, but there was also cloud cover and possible rain on the way. The streets were just dirt and the old buildings had only small lanterns lit. I could see some people were still awake and coming to their windows trying to figure out where the commotion was coming from, nosy humans.

I could see the forest just past some houses. If I can make it into the forest, I can much more easily hide. As I passed between two homes a dog picked up my scent. I turned back to it as it got ready to start barking. I quickly formed a bone in front of it. Luckily, the dog gladly took the offering and left me be. I continued to run more now.

This forest was thick, with tall trees, lots of moss, bushes, and greenery, I could also hear a stream up ahead. I was already exceptionally good at suppressing my magic but if I needed to use it, the water could help null its feeling.

Once I walked up the stream and felt I was far enough from the town, I decided to rest. My heavy bag falling to my side dropped to my knees to take a drink, it is beautifully clear and cold. I had a soft navy-blue cloak that was big enough to wrap myself in. I rested at the base of a big tree. With the flow of the river's sound, the light wind rustling the trees, and the Earth magic surrounding me, I fell into a deep slumber.

I was jolted awake; I could hear two kids running through the forest. I needed to pick myself up quickly and throwing my bag over my shoulders I started walking into the forest more. Kids would never go too far into the forest. These ones, however, kept getting closer, I could hear the rustling of the leaves that were picked up by their feet, the broken tree limbs from under their weight. They weren't scared to be heard and found, which tells me these are Vampire children.

I found a large enough tree so I could hide in its trunk. I cast an illusion, a shadow over myself so I would just look like the shadow of the tree. I heard them come closer. It was then I saw a few deer travel across the river.

"Look!" It was a young girl that spoke out first.

"Angela stay away, we're in the forest if a witch spots us first, they could cast a spell on us." Lies but I get the kid's concern, he was a young male and sounded too authoritative to be just any Vampire's kid.

"I know, but they're so pretty. Besides, if we see a witch, your uncle would just catch it."

"Maybe, but I think it will be better if we head back. Mother won't be pleased with us if we stay out here too long."

I could hear them turning around when I felt another form approach. Vampires generally give off a void feeling in the air, but this one was large, making me believe he was unequivocally strong.

"Don't you two know how dangerous it is to be out here?" I did not need to guess who that was, his accent, the age in his voice, the depth of his demand, it was Lord Gerard. Now I only wish I cast more than just an illusion. I have the strength to do it, but I wasn't worried about kids, but now one wrong move would give my position away.

"Uncle, Angela and I found some deer, do you think we could practice hunting them?" Hunting for sport, their golden play game.

"No Galen, not right now. The Trials for the witches are in a few days and I have matters to attend to." Probably have outsiders coming into his land.

The Trials, where caught witches are taken and told to perform complex skills to see where their rank falls, then sold to the highest bidder.

I took a quick glance back over at the deer, they were watching us and keeping their distance, but they hadn't run away. They must know I'm here; most animals don't fear us but with the Vampires here they won't approach.

A squirrel was coming down the tree and entered into my Shadow, disappearing with me, then I heard it, that slight foot rotation. Gerard knew I was here.

Thinking fast I dove out into the water, placing my hands on the water, and electrifying it. I tried keeping my magic contained because I could light the river up for miles, probably right into town, but I couldn't let him know how strong I was, too much was at stake. I glared back at one of the strongest Lords, with his crimson red eyes staring right back.

"I'll get her uncle!" The young kid started running towards me but stopped just at the edge of the water. "Come out witch, you won't be able to run from us!" I hate naive little kids, but if I did hurt him Gerard would have my head. I just kept the water charged.

I spoke out, never looking at the child but keeping a firm gaze on Gerard, "Listen I don't want any trouble, I am just a humble traveler passing through."

"If you belonged to someone, I might have contemplated it, but seeing as you have no owner, and that impressive offensive spell you just cast, I will not let you leave." The young female clung to his side as he walked to the edge of the water. "You two stay here."

"Uncle, what are you going to do?"

He looked down at the two, "Just watch, maybe you could learn a few things." They both smiled up at him and turned back to me.

"Come witch, don't make this hard on yourself."

"I never wanted to play hard, I just wanted to leave in peace." If I maneuvered my spell or cast the strength any higher, he would only want me more, this may have put me at a level two witch, at most, but if I do more he might think I have potential, then he would just want to keep me for himself.

I stepped back, "listen I don't have any intentions of going to the trials, just leave me be."

He stopped and spread out his arms, "then please stop me." He continued towards me.

I did the only thing I could think of, I gathered all the electricity in the water and shot it at him. As I cast out my arm, he charged at me, grabbing my wrist, and when I saw the lightning release from my hand it directly hit him in the chest. He did not falter, move, or seemed fazed by this feeble attempt, but I couldn't let him see my full strength.

He smiled at me but also seemed disappointed that the fight was over so soon. "Well, come on witch, let us go say Hi to the rest of the family." He held my wrist firm and dragged me back out of the water, I had no choice but to stumble out behind him. When we started heading out of the forest, I turned back around to see it empty, the deer had run off, they were free, something I would only now get to dream about.

***

He pushed me ahead of him and the young kids were at either of my sides. I could hear the morning bells play in the town. The Sun was starting to rise but it was still cloudy holding onto its rain, the town would be full of people, and once we start walking through, everyone's going to want a peek at the witch the Lord of their small tiny little lives had caught.

"Don't cause a scene, I don't need to deal with dead people."

"Well, unlike your kind, I don't kill for sport." I held my head up high, I may hide my power, but I will not act weak.

"If that is what you think, then you know nothing of our kind."

I looked up at him questionably, then turned back to the path, "I know enough."

Once we were about to step into the town, he grabbed my arm and dragged me through the streets. Looking more closely at him he was much taller, probably taller than the average man. His ash-coloured air was short but long enough to style, he had a strong jaw, with broad shoulders, so of course, the Lord of the land would have a handsome figure. He held himself up with strong authority, this is what the young kid was trying to imitate. He stared back at me, and I let our eyes meet for a moment, before continuing to stare forward again.

I saw a lengthy woman standing in the town square, she had long black straight hair and a pointed nose. The young kids ran over and hugged her from behind. When she turned around, she saw us walking up. She locked her eyes on mine, before turning to Gerard.

"What do you have here brother?" Her voice was quite soft compared to the coldness she sends off with her body.

"Witch, maybe a level two could be three, she was holding back."

"A witch that holds back generally has more to hide than just a simple level three." She was cunning, she knows how this works. "Tell me, witch, what is your name?"

"Angelic" I bowed my head just slightly, these two were royalty, and without proper treatment, they could hurt you in more ways than what is even imaginable.

"It is possible that she could be stronger, but I can't see her being anything more than a three," Gerard said.

"Well brother I guess we shall see in the Trials, now won't we." She peered down at me, then moved to let us pass.

Gerard nudged me forward and we continued over to the carriages, basically a cage being pulled by magic, on the other end of the square. The kids stayed with the women.

"If you do prove yourself to be stronger, I may let you stay here, I doubt you want to be sold into a poor merchant's house, or how about the games?"

"You're very charitable, my Lord." He smiled at my sarcasm.

"Tell me, would you have hurt those kids if I never came." He let go of my arm and faced me. Where was he going with this?

"I would not have bothered hiding if I planned on hurting them."

"I see, that was a Shadow spell was it not?"

"Was it?" I looked at him questionably.

"You're holding back, you're hiding either an extraordinary amount of power or at least a more impressive amount. I will test you, I caught you which means I get first rights to keep you, and if I don't see what I want I will sell you to any bidder." He then motioned for me to get into the carriage and shut the door.

"See you in a week Angelic."

I watched him as the carriage started to move forward. Once he was out of sight, I sat down waiting to arrive at a place that can bring a lot of suffering to my life.

My head was resting on the bars when I heard someone start hitting them. "Wake up!" I looked over to see the same Vampire with a scar, Rig was his name. I stood up, kind of shakily, dizzy from the ride.

"I knew there was more to you, *witch*." The way he says 'witch' was definitely in a non-pleasing way. We were nothing but a tool to them.

I stepped out of the carriage and got a quick look around. The Trials would be held in a stadium, it was quite large and can hold many spectators and bidders and wouldn't be surprised if there was some gambling.

As I was trying to look around, Rig grabbed my jaw, "eyes forward!" On instinct I charged my hand and grabbed him, he instinctively let me go, but came back with a vengeance, hitting me square across the face. Not hard enough to bring me to the ground but enough to make my head spin.

"You better watch yourself; you may be Lord Gerard' now, but right now you're in my yard, I make the rules." He then spat at me and started walking away. It was expected that I follow, and I did think for a moment not to, but that would only bring me more grievance.

The so-called 'yard' was literally just a large oval field filled with Vampire guards, and witches all over. Some were practicing spells on heavy objects, I could see some casting elemental spells, others were just sitting staring, waiting for the Trials. Rig had stopped in front of one of the small buildings, when he knocked on the door, a petite female with green eyes opened it up, she was a witch.

He pushed me forward, "she will be bunking with you and your crew." He then turned and walked away.

She immediately stuck her tongue out at him, childish but greatly amusing.

"Hi, I'm Lucia."

"Hello, I'm Angelic."

"Come in before we get pulled out onto the grounds." I hustled inside and she closed the door behind me.

There were four bunk beds, there were only three beds made, soon to be four.

"Please pick whichever unmade bed you would be most comfortable at." I looked at them all and picked the one furthest from the door, it was a bottom bunk, but I would rather stay away from that door.

"So, Angelic, how did you get caught?"

"You just like to jump into the personals, don't you?" I looked back at her as I sat on the edge of the bed.

"Sorry, a habit of mine."

"It's fine, I had a run-in with the Lord himself. Didn't really leave me with a choice." Her eyes grew wide, she knew what that meant, no one would touch me here, I would be 'safe' until the end of the Trials, but there were also other speculations.

"So, you must be like a class four or five!" She was excited almost a bit too much?

"You already asked me a personal question, I don't think it's fair you get two and I get none." I smiled at her in a teasing way.

"Sorry again, just my magic is weak, I can barely pass at a level 2, I'm going to be sold off to the crummiest, sketchiest, piece of garbage there is." She felt this truth very strongly.

"How long have you been here for?"

She looked up at the ceiling, and I now noticed I should be thankful I took a bottom bunk because once it starts raining, that is going to leak.

"I would say maybe two moons." I was a bit shocked for her to be here that long and only be a level two, usually, you can practice as much as you want before the games. "Everybody just kind of keeps to themselves, no one helps each other out. I was thinking you were maybe a level one or two like me because you didn't have one of those collars, but then you said Lord Gerard caught you, so now I'm not sure."

"You mean those godforsaken collars that cancel out our connection to the Earth?" Ultimately voiding our power unless given permission by our masters, created by our own kind. The garbage scum who thought of it should be murdered.

"Yeah, I had only seen one other person with it on, but even he says he's only a level three."

There aren't many as strong as me. They stayed at the Royals table, they didn't want freedom they wanted power, so they now get to grow their magic but have to serve a Royal family.

"Well, Lucia..." As much as I wanted to tell her I could probably kill everyone here and escape, I couldn't. I would be found again by stronger Vampires, maybe even high-level witches, and who knows the torture they would put me through then. "You see it was only by coincidence that I ran into Gerard, I'm only a level two maybe top three." Luckily witches were easier to lie to than a Vampire, they can see every change in your muscles as you talk to them, every eye twitch or movement, and if you lied to them and they knew, you might as well chop your own arm off.

She nodded and accepted my answer, "so do you want to go take a look around?"

"Honestly right now I want to sleep, I haven't slept much in the last couple of days."

"Ok, I'm heading out to practice on the levitation spells, you can come to join us anytime." I nodded at her, as she got up and left.

The place was basically a shack, and the rain was coming, probably here by tonight, and there was a charge in the air. I laid on my hard, moldy-smelling bed, wrapped my cloak around me, and fell asleep.

CHAPTER TWO

I dreamt of Doe eyes, they felt sorry for me, they knew what was in store. They ran into a meadow, the sun was shining, but out in the clearing were two young Vampires, they were hunting. I wanted to yell out at the deer to stop and go the other way, but I couldn't make a sound. I had chains on my wrists and a collar around my neck. I could do nothing but watch. They were closing in on the deer, they leaped towards them. I saw a deer get thrown to the ground, but before the young bloodsucker could bite into him, I was startled awake.

My cloak was on the ground, and it was cold, I could feel the dampness from outside. It was a heavy shower, but no one was inside. There was yelling from outside that made me wake up. I got up and opened the door, taking heavy showers. Usually I would just cast protection around me to keep me dry, but I can't now. I looked up and saw the dark clouds, they won't let up anytime soon. I could have just gone back inside and not worry what others were doing, but from what I could tell everyone was at the levitation area, and the Vampires were just watching a show. I couldn't abandon someone that could be a friend, we had just met, but she had good qualities, I could feel it in her aura.

I lifted the hood of my cloak and walked out to the crowd. As

I got closer, I noticed there was some cheering and booing. They were competing, that was an obvious, dangerous thing about competition, people died. Swerving my way into the crowd I came to the front and saw the nightmare in front of me. Lucia was competing against another female, she was larger than Lucia, not hard to do with her petite size, she definitely had more power. They were both standing in front of two weights trying to levitate two hundred pounds. This was a level three-act, Lucia was not, but neither was this other woman, their power would snap and reverberate back, don't think enough to kill but it will hurt, a lot. With the Trials in a few days, she may not even be healed by then.

I turned to a short man beside me, "Hey, do you know what's going on here?"

"Oh, hello, you must be new, Viera challenged Lucia for food tokens." I could tell he was older, only a small amount of gray hair, but he seemed wiser than the age he portrayed.

"That's a thing?" Shit, I forgot about food, how the hell does this place work.

"Oh yes, we only get a token a day, and Viera will try to get at least one or two more. She will save them before the Trials."

"But just because you eat more, trying to have more energy, doesn't mean your magic will be any stronger." He smiled at me.

"Yes, that is true, but the younger ones don't know that. Tell me, what level are you?"

"Seems to be my most sought-after question here."

"I'm sorry if it makes you feel uncomfortable."

"No not at all it's fine, I would range closer to a three."

He grabbed my shoulder, "then maybe you could stop this, you know what will happen to them if they continue for too long."

I looked back at Lucia, she was struggling, and even in this rain, she was sweating. "Sadly, I do."

The man then raised his hand, "Here! We have a new challenger."

Everyone stopped to look at us, Lucia turned too and noticed it was me, she looked exhausted, so did the other women, they were close, maybe too close.

The man pushed me forward, "this woman here, I say if she can lift one of the weights the challenge will be canceled, and everyone walks away." I saw a few of the Vampires come in closer, I didn't see Rig, maybe he was on break?

"Who is she?" Viera was panting heavily but she tried to act tough.

Lucia spoke up, "that's Angelic, she just got here." She was trying to catch her breath as she spoke.

"Alright then if she wants to compete to end the competition that's fine by me, but if she fails I get all her tokens." Well, that won't happen, but I also really didn't want to get involved.

I walked up, feeling the wet grass soaking through my shoes, it made me feel more connected to the water element. It was a nice feeling before I stood in front of the weight just a few feet ahead of me. I looked over at Lucia and she smiled lightly. Viera had her arms crossed and was smirking, their power was starting to regenerate, and they were getting out of the danger area.

"You guys do know you both are going to fail right?"

"Ha! You're a coward if you don't want to do this then just say so!" She walked up beside me, faced the two-hundred-pound weight, stretched out her arms, and hoisted up. To be fair the rock did move, not off the ground, but rolled a bit. She was in an instant sweat, but stood tall and looked back at me, "Your turn newbie."

I turned back away from her and looked at this thing. I could take it and throw it at her, but that gave everyone the wrong impression, and I can't lose to her because I didn't want to lose all my food tokens. Contemplating this, I looked out, and I saw the young kid, Galen, he was with that Vampire guard Rig. So, they were watching, but what was the kid doing here?

"Are you going to do this or what?" She spoke irritatingly at me. I barely glanced at her.

I decided to use two arms, like her, to make it seem more believable that I am merely a level three. I hoisted the weight up but only a few inches, I didn't need to show off, even a level three could lift higher, but I don't want to show as much as I don't have to.

People were in awe, they knew now I was permanently in the level three slot, and they wouldn't challenge me, nor Lucia because they knew she was with me. I let the weight drop back on the ground.

"Whatever" and Viera turned around and started walking back to her own shack I assumed.

Lucia came over and engulfed me in a hug. "Thank you so much! I would have lost everything."

I pulled her away from me but only to look at her, "Lucia you could have lost more than just food tokens, you could have injured yourself beyond healing. You do know that right?"

She looked away from me, "Yeah, I know that, but if someone challenges you and you decline you have to give them half of what the winner would have won, and I couldn't spare any more than I had already lost." I couldn't argue that, nor could I challenge the stupidity of this whole thing.

I looked over to see Galen coming this way, peculiarly though, Rig did not follow. "Lucia, go back to the cabin. I want you to go there and rest. You need to recharge before you try to use spells again."

"Ok, you're right." She left and started to head back.

The crowd was mostly broken apart now, I watched as some went to bed and others went to other practice rounds. The rain was lighting up a bit but not enough that I wanted to stay outside.

"Hello Master Galen, what do I owe this visit for?" I turned towards him. He was nearly my height but still a bit shorter, with more golden blond hair. He had a lithe frame like his mother, he would never grow up to be built like his uncle.

"I came to see how you were doing. I saw your performance, you were holding back on my uncle, weren't you?"

I sighed, "there was no point in fighting Lord Gerard, he is too strong for even the strongest of my kind."

"Couldn't say that you're wrong, but it would have been more entertaining to see a strong witch cast a strong spell." His answer was peculiar.

"Have you never seen a real fight with a witch?"

"Not in battle, if there is a battle with one of them, I would not be allowed to be around. Too dangerous, my mother would say."

"Do you like fighting?"

"No, I just think magic is interesting. The abilities it can be used for. All the mages back home don't bother me because I'm young, even when all I ask to see is something small." Kids got a bit too curious about magic, and could hurt him if he's not careful.

"Here." I bent down in front of him and opened my hand on the ground. I grew the small flower into a beautiful blossoming one. I removed my hand and let him see. He wasn't looking at me but at the flower. He reached out to touch it.

"Bah!" I laughed as he jumped back, "Sorry kid I couldn't help it."

"That's not funny!"

"Sorry" I stopped quickly before I could get into too much trouble.

He came back over but was smiling, he thought it was funny too. He reached down and plucked the flower.

"Be sure to put it in some water, it'll last longer." He nodded then turned and ran back towards Rig. God, I hope he doesn't tell his uncle, or worse his mother, she's a terrifying-looking lady.

I saw Rig lead the kid out of the courtyard. This was my

queue so that I could leave this mushy, rainy land and head back inside. Some people were staring at me on my way back, no doubt they saw what I did but I'm not their friend, I'm their competition for the best slot, the coziest home, or Master I should say. I couldn't afford to be weak here or at least weak enough that I couldn't defend myself. More importantly, when Lucia wakes up, we'll need to get some food.

I got back to our living quarters and noticed the three others were in their beds. Lucia was snoring away in her top bunk. I took off my wet clothes and found a simple gown to wear. Once my clothes were hung up to dry, I slipped into bed and fell right back to sleep.

I heard a few people rustling and started getting up and going out. I felt my stomach gurgle and knew my rest was over, my stomach wouldn't let me sleep without being sated. When I got up, I saw Lucia just waking up. She was tired from yesterday's events, but this doesn't look like her first time. How many times has she come close to death?

"Hey Lucia, time to eat yet?"

She smiled over at me, "You bet, I'm starving!" We heard a knock on the door, and we both looked over at the same time. "Who would be knocking here?" I shrugged and walked to the door.

Opening the door, it was the young Vampire from the town who stood in front of me, Kai I believe.

"Hello" I nodded at him in respect.

"Angelic, I got these for you." He pulled out five tokens.

"Good timing, we were just about to head out to grab some food." I smiled at him and let him place the tokens in my hands, you never take something from a Vampire.

"Have a good day then." He walked away without much of a goodbye, maybe I was wrong to think my charms worked on him?

"Great, now we can go without delays." Lucia then ran out in front of me.

I quickly caught up to her. Looking around, the sun was beautifully shining and rising in the distance. The birds were also more vocal this morning. I think most of the Vampires were in the cafeteria, a few outside. Sun doesn't hurt them much unless they're starving, and I doubt guards starve.

We came up to a larger building, inside was a lineup of witches waiting their turn. It looked like they were feeding us chili with bread. Perfectly fine with me, after a wet night having something warm would be nice.

We came up behind a few others and waited our turn. When we got our chili, I was surprised that it even smelled good, I truly expected mush or just bile in a bowl. The bread was fresh, and we were able to get a hot drink. We found a couple of empty seats and sat down, I noticed Viera talking to that other level three. He did have the collar on, I wonder if I'll end up with one now.

"Don't worry you won't." I looked at her like she had three heads, "You won't get a collar, it's because his captures wanted him to wear it, they didn't want him to try and escape."

"I see, well that's good then." I turned to my food and one bite I was hooked; it was actually good!

Lucia was laughing at me, "Don't worry we all think the same thing when we first get here."

"I think I get why people compete for the tokens now." She smiled and continued eating.

I was almost done when I felt a familiar presence, "Shit." Lucia looked at me then to the door. She saw the young kid come in and noticed he was looking around, but I think she was more impressed that I noticed his presence so soon.

He was coming over now and practically behind me. Lucia tilted her head at me, and I turned to see him standing and gleaming.

"Master Galen, you look to be in a good mood today, to what can we owe the pleasure?"

"Mother told me I could come and watch. I decided since

you're my uncle that I'd stick with you and watch how you get ready." This just got more complicated, I wasn't planning on practicing, at least, not in view of everyone else.

"Well, you see, I wasn't completely planning on practicing very much, because I plan to help Lucia with getting her ready for the Trials." I smiled at her hoping she would just agree. Luckily, she caught on.

"Oh yes, Angelic is stronger than I, and figured she could help me get ready." She smiled at him.

"That's ok, could even be better really."

"Can it?" I didn't mean to state it in a disappointing tone, but he didn't seem to notice.

"Yeah, it'll be neat to see two witches' practice, besides, I don't really care about others here. You're going to be living at our house."

"How can you be so certain?"

"My uncle knows, " Rig told him about the two-hundred-pound weight competition. He knows you have more to offer." I sighed, not good news. At least being at some mediocre Vampires place I could probably escape but being at the Royal manor, I would have no chance.

"Alright then," I turned back to Lucia, "Ready to go then?"

"Certainly," she got up with her dishes and I followed her out.

Others were starting to follow suit and go to different stations, Lucia started to head to one station before I stopped her.

"Listen Lucia, I need you to do something before we practice offensively." She looked at me quizzically. I looked around and saw a huge tree! He was perfect. I led them both over and touched the tree and closed my eyes. I could feel everything he has seen, the protection he offers from the elements, the birth of animals in his limbs, he has immense pride in his full form, but right now he is going into slumber but accepts my greetings.

"Angelic, what are you doing?"

"This tree will be perfect; Lucia I want you to tell me everything you can about this tree."

"Oh umm, Ok." She came over and copied what I did. "Well, he expels more masculine energy, he wants to be a protector."

"Yes, how old are you?"

"Hmmm, maybe 80 years."

"He's over a hundred." Lucia looked up at the tree, seeing his falling leaves.

"Now I want you to take the energy and expel it, go as far as you can, and tell me what you feel."

"I don't think I've done that before."

"I figured that's why I got you to read the tree first, take that same feeling and reach out." She nodded at me.

She sat down and put her hands on the ground, "I feel you, and I feel something strange, I can't even describe it."

"Excellent, I call it 'the void' , it's what his kind sends off. That's how I knew he entered earlier."

"Wait you knew I entered and where I was before I even saw you!" He looked so intense like he had never heard of this before.

"Angelic, that's quite the skill I can barely project it out far enough to get past him."

"I've had a lot of practice, and Galen please try to avoid telling people. I needed Lucia to learn this skill because it will help protect her during the trials."

"I won't, but that's so cool. I don't even think many other witches and mages do it at the palace." I nodded at him.

"How can this help me?"

"Think about it Lucia, if you knew where your attacker was at all times, then they can never surprise you. If you can read this tree, you can read those around you. You will know how strong they are compared to you. Some level fives don't even know this skill. It is quite simple, it's all about awareness. So, for now, I want you to sit here and practice. I'll come up to you from different angles and you'll point me out. Maybe I'll even get Galen here too, it is good to learn how his kind feels."

"That's amazing! I can't wait to try this." She rested against the tree and started to work up her magic, I could feel it start to radiate from her.

"Alright Galen you go out and start coming towards her and once she points you out stop and try again. Our goal is to tap her on the shoulder, if we do, she loses."

"Okay!" He then ran out into the field, and I followed shortly.

CHAPTER THREE

We had done this until mid-day, but I could tell Lucia was getting tired and we took a break. Lucia left to get us some water and Galen left to go home and eat. The tree and silence were a nice break. I could see Viera and that other level three working together. They were definitely friends and there would be trouble in the competition. Reaching out I could tell Lucia was on her way back and when she was close enough, I opened my eyes.

"So, how long did it take you to notice me coming towards you?"

"You never left my radar," I smiled at her.

"So, you're quite strong, aren't you? I promise Angelic I won't tell anyone, but you keep to yourself but have all this knowledge."

"I was a traveler Lucia, I read a lot, I heard many stories, and I have met many other witches. You learn more on the road, being stuck as a slave will weaken you." She looked sad, like a part of her that she'll never even get to explore. "Why don't we sit here for a bit and just relax?" She nodded and took a seat beside me.

It was a while before the sun started setting, which was good, we had been practicing off and on all day. We were about to go back to our quarters before I noticed Galen coming back, what is he doing here at nightfall?

"Hey" he waved over and ran towards us; he used a bit of his vampire speed this time. "What are we going to do now?"

"We were actually about to go back and rest until tomorrow. Lucia will need her strength tomorrow."

"I will?"

"Yes, we will work on some offensive tomorrow." She smiled

"Wow, that's going to be so cool! I can't wait to see it! Is there anything that you can teach us now? Any stories?"

"I agree, you said you learned from other witches, what else have you learned?" Lucia seemed just as deeply interested as the kid.

"Alright, one thing then you go home, and we go rest."

"Agreed!" they said at the same time.

"We all know there are level fives, that's our top-level," they both nodded. "Well, there *was* another, but they were not rated, they were so powerful that the Royals decided to kill them then try to tame them." They were leaning in both enthralled in this story. "It's said that they emit so much power that their aura becomes visible. Those spells could be so strong that they could kill and level towns. Even Royals could be killed by their spells. They always had one thing though when they emitted their power, and that was their deep-coloured pink eyes. They believe some are still alive but hiding, maybe in the deserts, or even under our own noses, but they're so skilled you would just never know." I let the story sink in, and it was Galen who spoke up first.

"Have you seen one before?"

"I have actually, she was murdered, I was very young and barely remember but it was a power that Vampires were afraid of, so they killed her for it."

"But it sounds so cool!"

"Yes, but that type of magic would kill you. You have to be

very careful young Master, your uncle could take a hard hit, but you're still young and could be killed."

"I know, mom tells me that all the time."

"I think it's time we rest." We all stood up and we started walking back towards the quarters.

I saw that level three and Viera came out around another cabin.

"Well, well, well, look what the cat threw up." They stood in front of us, and I noticed he wasn't wearing his collar.

"Where's your leash?" I snapped.

"Don't be a cocky newbie."

"Conner, Viera, we're just heading back to our quarters, and the young Galen here is heading home, please just let us through." Very diplomatic of Lucia.

"We couldn't care less about that little squirt but you two I think it's time you hand over your tokens." Connor lifted his hands and a ball of flame erupted from his palms.

I stood in front of them both, "listen we have no interest in giving you anything, and if you start shooting fireballs around, you'll burn everything around you. Now get out of our way." I started to emit more power just enough to give a good warning. Their stance stiffened, getting ready for me to do something, but I blinked and relaxed. I felt this before, looking at Lucia she now felt him too.

"I can see we are all getting along here," Gerard spoke behind them and they jumped nearly out of their skin. They fell to their knees.

"I am sorry Lord Gerard, we never meant to harm your nephew, but we have fair game against the two witches," Connor spoke.

"I obviously know the rules, now get out of the way." They stood up, looked back at us then ran off towards their cabin. "Galen, what are you doing, it's nightfall." He glanced up at me before returning to Galen.

"I know Uncle, but I didn't want to miss anything! Ava was

telling us about a story of a witch with so much power that even vampires were scared of it!" Ava? Seems I earned a nickname.

"Had she now? And what did she say?"

"How they could level a whole town!" He threw out his arms to express the explosion. This seemed to make him smile.

"Well, that is true, anything else she cared to share?" He was looking at me and I could tell he was studying me.

Galen put his fingers to his chin, "Oh! She said their spell could kill a Royal. Though I'm not sure about that, I've never seen any witch come close to killing a Royal on their own." He turned back to him.

"Believe it, they are most dangerous, I've seen it. Even almost killed me once long ago." Galen' eyes widened.

Galen turned back towards me, I bowed in respect, mostly for show in front of Gerard, I don't need that trouble towards me.

"Uncle, can I come back tomorrow?" Gerard lifted one of his eyebrows and dare I say it was cute. I did a little sigh on the inside even thinking about it.

"Of course, I don't see why not."

Galen smiled up at his uncle. "I'll see you guys tomorrow, then run off towards the outer gates." How I wish I could waltz out of this place, without the chances of being hunted later.

"Careful what stories you speak of, wouldn't want to be sending the wrong impression." He then turned and walked away. Lucia and I both bowed as he left then we turned to each other.

"He is so intense! I actually felt him coming sooner than Galen."

"He takes up a lot of space."

"That's scary Ava, I don't know if I could handle that." I looked at her. "What? Ava is a nice nickname; it works for you." I rolled my eyes and walked back to our cabin, or more appropriate our shack. She followed up behind me. Tomorrow we will be working on her element, and she will need all the rest she can get.

Like clockwork, Galen met us outside the cafeteria this time. "Good morning, Master Galen." I smiled at him, and we continued towards our tree.

"Ava, you think I'll really be able to do it?"

"Of course, if I didn't, I wouldn't bother teaching you."

"What are we doing?" Galen was excited, this is why he was coming around.

"I'm going to teach her the same thing I threw at your uncle."

"Oh cool! That looked like it would have hurt."

"For you, it would have stunned you at least for a couple of hours. No effect on him though."

As we got to our spot, under the big tree, I noticed Galen had brought some things, "Galen, why do you have a book bag?"

"I brought lunch, this way I don't have to leave, and I thought maybe after practicing so much you would be hungry too" Oh great, extra treatment, not what we need to deal with here. The girls back at our quarters even got jealous and ignored us when we got in.

"Awe thanks, Master Galen." Lucia obviously didn't notice danger in it. Oh, hell with it, everyone was already against us.

"Yeah, thanks, Galen." He smiled at us and took a seat against the tree.

"Alright, Lucia I need you to stand quite still. Stretch out your arms, palms up, and close your eyes." She did as she was told. "Now I need you to feel the air, look for the charge in the air, unfortunately, it'll be harder since we have clear skies, but it is there. Harder technically isn't a bad thing either, it will help you practice your focus."

"I can feel a tickle almost."

"That's exactly it, focus on it, charge your fingers." I could see her focusing in and I could even see a small charge forming. I tapped her hand and the charge was released , sending a small shock to both of us. It startled her enough she took a step back.

"That was neat," she stretched her neck and resumed her

position. We did this for the next few hours. Galen never moved but watched intently.

"Alright, guys, why don't we have lunch?"

"That sounds great, I'm starving."

Galen pulled out two sandwiches and a drink for himself. The sandwiches were filled with turkey, lettuce, mayo, and was just heaven! Damn, he was dragging me in. Unfortunately, I think they both were.

"Ava, do you have any more stories?" I looked over at Galen, but Gerard' words came back to me.

"Actually, I have a question for you Galen." He looked over at me, raising his head from his drink. "I haven't seen a witch with your uncle, does he not have any?"

"Oh, he does, sort of, it's complicated. He has none that belong to him strictly, but they belong to other Royals at the palace, but if he wished he could use one of them."

"Why hasn't he gotten one of his own?"

"He said, in the past, it was because they were too weak. He's strong, stronger than most Vampires if not all, and he said they would just be a burden on him." He looked at me with sadness in his eyes.

"What is it, Galen?"

"Well, he just hadn't expressed much interest in you, that was until yesterday." That goddamn story! I screwed myself, but that was my mother not me. I just figured it would be good for Galen to know that witches can be extremely powerful. Not many of us but some.

"I see, well I guess I should be careful then."

"Ava, I want you to be in the palace, I'm trying to convince my mother to buy you if Uncle Gerard doesn't keep you."

"Galen, don't you worry about me, I can take care of myself, but Lucia, she needs help, try to keep her safe."

"Thanks, Ava, but you're more valuable than me." I shook my head at her.

"You have strength, just weren't guided correctly. You have

class three in you, but I just don't have the time to get you there before the Trials. You'll have to work ridiculously hard at the few lessons I can give before then."

She reached out and touched my hand, "Thank you Angelic, truly." She pulled back and stood up, "Ok then! I'm going to get back to practicing." But then she stopped, and we all looked over noticing the coming presence.

It was Galen' mother, the scary woman walking in all her pride over towards us. He stood up and I followed. Lucia and I bowed our heads, when she stopped in front of us, we stood up straight.

"Mother, is there something wrong?"

"No, my love, but you need to come home, there are many new people showing up for the new trials and I would prefer you in the safety of the manor than out here with these... beings." She didn't seem sour about us, she used us just like anyone else.

"Oh, but mother! Can I at least stay the rest of today! Please!" Just like any other little kid, ignoring the safety warnings from the parents for his own pleasures.

"Galen I don't think that would be a good idea."

"My Lady, I can keep him safe." I put my arm to my chest, "I'll keep him safe in this compound along with the capable guards. No one will bother him, and I'll be sure to escort him to the outside gates.

"How can I trust you; you have no ownership."

"Call it a return of the favor he gave us with the excellent food he provided." She seemed amused by this but to be fair, that was the best sandwich I have ever eaten.

She looked back at Galen who was giving the biggest puppy eyes I had ever seen, now he's the one I need to learn the charming look from. "Fine, but if anything comes to harm him, you will see the red *witch*."

"Is a threat I'll take very seriously; I know you are capable of many traumas." She smirked at me before returning to her son.

"Gale will come and pick you up by nightfall."

"Ok mother." He went and hugged her. She accepted it gladfully then walked back out.

"So, you're like my own personal bodyguard right now Ava." He had a big smile on his face.

"Don't get used to it, remember we're helping Lucia get through these trials."

"I know." He then returned to his seat, and I went back to teach Lucia for the remainder of the day.

CHAPTER FOUR

By nightfall we were all tired, I practiced extreme control. Trying to spark one blade of grass, they never noticed it, but it made me tired to focus for so long. Lucia was getting better, practicing the next couple of days will get her well prepared for the Trials.

"Alright Lucia I got to bring Galen back to the front gate, I'll meet you back at our bunks."

"Sounds good," she turned to Galen, "I guess I won't see you for three days, be safe, and say hi before I leave for a new home."

He hugged her, "I will!" He let her go and she walked back towards our small little home. Suppose that's what it turned into after these short days of getting to know each other.

"Alright Master Galen, I will be your guard today, let's head out shall we." I spread out my arm for him to lead ahead. I think even though I'll miss him being around a bit, his curiosity about how things work helps me remember my knowledge on the subject. Good for the Trials coming up.

We were almost to the gates when I felt Kai coming out of the building next to the entrance.

"Sorry young Master, but Gale hasn't shown up yet."

"But if I don't get home before the sun sets, mom will freak out." He was worried about his mother's anger, and I don't blame him.

"I'm sorry." Kai bowed.

"I guess I will just wait to see if he shows up." Galen went to take a seat next to the gate and I followed beside him.

It was now completely dark outside, and there were no signs of him or any messages from the palace. I looked around and saw one of those Royal carriages. I got up and went to the building, knocking on the door Kai answered.

"Yes?"

"Kai we both know he needs to get home, or the likelihood of an uproar is high, mages will think they could exchange his life for their freedom, you know which ones I'm thinking of." He nodded in agreement. "We need to get him home, you have a Royal carriage there, I can pull it with my magic, you sit inside with him." He looked at the carriage then back at Galen.

"I didn't want to, but I thought this might happen." He came out and shut the door behind him. "Ok, you go get the carriage and I'll open the gates." I nodded at him and went to grab it.

Big, bulky and ugly were my only thoughts but I could put him inside and hide his presence and my magic so that no one will know we are even passing through. I got in the driver's seat and raised it up and pushed it forward with ease. "Wow Ava, I didn't know you had this kind of skill."

I smiled and put a finger to my lips, "Shhh let's not tell anyone." I winked at him before motioning him to get in by opening the door without having to move in the slightest. They got in and shut the door. I pulled the carriage forward and we were off down the road to the Palace.

I could easily abandon them, out here in the middle of the forest, it would be too easy, but the little bastard caught me in his charm, now I'm stuck. I'll make sure he gets home safe but after the Trials, I have no promises to him.

I could hear the crows calling, they were the eyes of the forest. I could tell there were hunters, hiding, waiting. My spell was working well. I threw us off their trail by miles, they were heading the wrong way.

After a few more miles I saw something, it was another carriage.

"Oh no, Kai stayed with Galen, I think I saw Gail's Carriage."

"Don't you dare leave us!"

"I promise I won't be far, but I need to check it out." He grunted in acknowledgment.

I got down from my seat and the carriage stayed level. As I got closer, I could feel his presence, which meant he was still alive. I got to the door and knocked, no answer. Opening it I saw him on the floor, unconscious. "Shit."

"Kai, I need you!" I yelled back and Galen and he were with me in a moment. We need to get him back; he won't live long staying out here alone.

"Do you think this Carriage still works?" Kai asked.

I took a quick look, "yes you are right, get in this one and will take this one back." We had to move quickly. My magic was only on our carriage, we were too exposed right now being outside.

As they got in and repositioned Gale, I lifted the carriage to an even level. I started to move the old spell to this one, but it was too late. I felt a direction change in the air. God damn Vampires why do they notice every little thing? I got up in the driver's seat, turned this thing around, and jolted forward. I needed us to move fast.

I felt three different voids coming close to us. They didn't have good intentions, that's for sure. I asked the trees to slow them down using their roots. They gladly obliged and I could tell they started slowing down. I only needed us close enough to get noticed. Then it hit me, I could warn Gerard that Galen was in trouble, he would take no time to find us. I focused and pushed out my thoughts, I looked forward, further and further, until I found him. "Help us!" Is all I spoke to him. He would get it and I wouldn't have to show off more than the few spells that I had.

They were starting to get closer; I caught a glimpse of one. He jumped out, reaching out towards the door. I threw out an electrical shock, this would stun him at least for a moment. There were others gaining, then I had to halt us, there were three in front of us, and a few coming up behind. I got off the carriage.

"Galen do not come out, and Kai you stay inside in case someone sneaks past."

"I can help!" That was from Galen

"Just do as you told Galen!" He never spoke back, and the rudeness in my voice was very much against the rules, but I had to keep him safe, for both our lives.

They were closing in, screw this, I circled the whole carriage in a wall of flame. This was a big spell for Vampires to see. It even made them stop, only for a second though. Then they were in view. They were assassins, and they won't stop until they get to their target.

"Stay back!"

"That's some impressive magic for what we were told was a weak witch. Still defensive magic though, what do you get that can actually hurt us?" He mocked me, he dared me to hit him with something harder.

I charged my hands and this time it would be harder, it would kill him, which I knew for sure. As he smiled and came closer, I stopped and stood straight up. I smiled back at him, then turned towards the front where Gerard already killed the other three. The assassin quickly noticed and ran off back into the woods. Gerard didn't follow but just came towards me.

"Are you going to lower your wall, or just drain yourself out?" Honestly, I barely noticed, but I did what he expected and sizzled out the flame. "Impressive for someone who gave out such a petty charge the other day." He smiled then turned towards the carriage. Before he could open the door, I opened it for him. It barely fazed him, but it had slightly and that made it very satisfying.

"Uncle Gerard," Galen jumped into Gerard' arms, and he was

actually smiling at Galen, happy that he was alive, almost worth all the trouble just to see a genuine smile coming from his lips. Lips that I must stop thinking about right now before I picture those on mine.

Another carriage with more guards came close. Galen' mom then stepped out and he ran to her. He hugged her and she held him close. She got him into the carriage, looked at me, nodded, then climbed back inside.

"I think you'll do just fine." I turned back to Gerard.

"What?"

"I don't need another power junkie; I need someone who will use their head. You have those talents. I look forward to seeing how you play the Trials."

"Play them, my Lord?"

He smiled down at me, "Kai, grab a few other guards and we will escort Miss Angelic back to the compound."

"You're coming?"

"I don't trust that you wouldn't try to run now that Galen is safe." I couldn't argue with that, and he knew it. He smiled at the win then pulled something out from his pocket. It was one of the collars. Well, there goes my thought of escape with a lower-class Vampire.

He wrapped it around my neck and locked it. When it turned on, I felt it, the void, the cut off; actually, it hurt a lot. "You know it would be safer walking through this forest if I could at least use my magic."

"True," he then pulled out a device and pushed a button and I was filled again with the flow of energy. I sighed in relief; he was watching me closely when I turned back to him. "Well let's get going." He headed off in front and I was behind him followed by a few of his guards.

We arrived back at the compound and once I got back to my quarters I fell into my bed and instantly fell asleep. Luckily, he didn't turn this thing back on, maybe because he knew I needed to defend myself while I was here, but now everyone knows I am more powerful than I let on.

I woke up to an empty cabin, which was good, I didn't really feel like explaining myself to Lucia right now. I felt the collar around my throat, it was the same thickness and texture all the way around except for the clasp where his blood would be required, damn royalty mages.

I tried heating it, burning it off, but the spell only ricochet back at me and instead, I burnt my hand. Seeing the scorch marks on my palms, I watched it heal instantly turning back to my skin tone. Fast healing is usually a Vampire trait but some of us have a knack for it. I lifted my head up in time to see Lucia walk in.

"How are you feeling?" She didn't get too close.

I sighed, "I'm fine." She then came to sit next to me.

"You know, at least it's black, it'll go with any outfit." I looked at her in bewilderment, she was smiling, almost laughing. It was contagious and we both started laughing. She stood up, "Come on I bet you're hungry." She reached out her hand and I grabbed it. She hoisted me up and we headed out to the cafeteria.

It was quiet in the cafeteria later in the day. Lucia had already eaten so she just watched me.

"How have you been practicing today?"

"I was able to shoot at a target." She was quite proud, and I don't blame her, not an easy task in such a short period of time.

"One more day after today." I put my utensil down, I wasn't even sure how these trials went.

"I don't think you have much to worry about, that's if Gerard makes you take them at all."

"Oh, he is, that's for sure." Thinking back to last night. Yeah, he definitely was not going to give me a pass on this.

"I don't think Galen will be coming anymore so let's make sure we show him something 'very cool' for him." Lucia used quotations as she spoke for Galen, he was an interesting Vampire child, most don't care for our kind unless they want something.

"I agree," I got up and we headed back to our spot, and we wouldn't leave there until the Trials.

Today was the day of the Trials and it was cloudy and going to rain. This worked in my favor if I needed to use certain skills. The guards came around collecting everyone and brought us into the stadium. We were underneath the stands in different cells. I could hear cheering and lots of yelling outside. I could see others all around and noticed Viera and Connor were in the same cell. Also, the gentleman from when I first arrived, I think Lucia said his name was Ralph?

Lucia was sitting on one of the beds, shaking like a leaf. I sat next to her and put my arm around her. I warmed us up, I knew it was nerves, but it was able to settle her a bit.

"Thanks," she eased into the warmth until we heard banging on different bars, and some witches started walking past us.

It was Rig who opened our cell door. "Let's go." He motioned for us to get out and follow everyone.

We followed the others out into the field, and when we entered the arena, it was quite overwhelming, there was a mixture of humans and Vampires in the stands. They were noisy and came to see a show, or at least see if any of us were actually interesting. I noticed Gerard in a different booth area, along with Galen and his mother. There was also another woman, sitting with Gerard, great he has a lover. I really need to stop thinking like that. Before I could get it out of my head Gerard noticed my staring and locked eyes with me. I turned toward Lucia before I let it linger too long.

"You ready?"

"As ready as I'm going to be." She gave a weak smile then squeezed my hand. There were probably about fifteen of us all lined up.

A male Vampire came out from another entrance, he was a higher-class Vampire, broad, tall, the kind that kills. He came out and faced the Royals first.

"We bow to our Royal family, who keep us safe in these

times." He gave a bow, and everyone in the stands also turned to bow. We followed in motion. "My name is Gary, and I will be your speaker today. Now, I give you our contestants, as you can tell we have two higher class witches. It should be interesting to see what they can pull off." The crowd cheered. "The rest are a mixture of level ones and twos. Everyone is up for bidding except for the two unless their captures decide not to take them." More cheering, this crowd was easily amused. "We will start with the individual testing. Viera, why don't you come up front and show us what you can do?"

He moved aside and she walked up in front. There were different targets in front of her, some looking like people, bullseye targets, different weights. She reached out and levitated the hundred-pound weight and threw it at the bullseye target. The target shattered into pieces. She then bowed to the Royal family and moved back in line. The crowd clapped, and so did Connor, happy for his little prodigy, I'm sure.

Gary clapped then called out another name. They moved to a target and tried shooting it with electricity but it sizzled and died before it reached the target. The next one was a female, I remember seeing her a couple times. She moved over to the center of the stage. Holding her hands out she produced a beautiful light, this was an excellent spell for humans, but vampires won't find it useful. It went on for a few others, some more impressive, some not at all. Then he came back and called for Lucia.

I turned to her quickly, "Push the two-hundred pound weight as far as you can."

"What why?"

"Trust me!" She walked to the front quickly. I knew she was practicing with electricity, but she needs to save it for when she really needs it.

She went to the front and faced the heavyweights. She focused in then released a high amount of energy force and knocked back the two-hundred-pound weight. It even went back a few feet, that's more impressive than Viera's little show, but this also shows buyers she can move heavy objects and that she has the potential to be a class three. She walked back towards me smiling.

"Galen was impressed." She looked up and Galen was clapping at her display.

"He is so sweet."

"You did well..." I heard Connor's name get called and he moved to center stage.

He turned back towards me before he engulfed all of the straw figures in flame. Everyone cheered and Galen looked very impressed. Maybe I was jealous?

Gary spoke out, "Alright, that will burn for a while. Now I give you Angelic. She was caught by our own Lord, it will be interesting to see what she pulls off after that last display." He looked at me with studying eyes.

As I took my place in the center everyone was staring, waiting to see what a class 3 could do. I shook my head, if only they knew the truth. I looked at Connors burning figures, so I decided to do something not too crazy but enough to be impressive. I suffocated the flames, you can't see anything except the flames diminishing. It surrounded the flames killing it into nothing but a cloud of smoke. I stood up and bowed at the Royal family before returning to my post.

"I think we got a bit of rivalry going on, but at least the flames are out, right folks." They all cheered out, but Gerard didn't look impressed, I don't think I'm getting bonus points. "Now we will test their skills on protection. They will each get an item to protect and will need to protect it for ten minutes, along with trying to destroy their competitions." The crowd cheered for entertainment.

Guards then came out holding what looked like large eggs. When I got past mine it was probably about ten pounds and quite large.

"Everyone spread out." Everyone chose a portion of the wall.

I decided not to move. "I see someone's going on the less protection route." Everyone laughed, but I could see Gerard was a bit more interested, unfortunately, the women beside him kept trying to distract him. Damn it I need to get that out of my head. I could see Galen was enthralled with everything, so that made this a little more fun.

"And Begin!"

Nobody moved, even Connor didn't move from his spot. I just stood there expecting this. No one would go on the offense and just be at a standstill. Then there were guards that came out, they started going after some of us. So that's how they break the ice. I looked up to see some people standing and cheering, yelling at the guards to 'kill the egg'. Savages I swear. One was coming towards me, it was Kai.

"Angelic, be prepared."

"For what?" I looked at him, daring him to come at me. He didn't move, it was quite entertaining really. I noticed there were many other eggs destroyed, except Connors and Ralphs, I looked for Lucia but she was already standing off to the side, when did Lucia lose hers?

Someone tried coming up behind me, but I immediately threw up my hands and set up a flame barrier around myself and the egg. It pushed them back, they may heal quickly but burning in the name of a game wasn't on their agenda.

Gary yelled out, "I see now why she never moved. This looks to be the same spell Connor used during the individual assessments. What will she do now."

"Come on Angelic this won't stop us," Kai shouted.

I smiled at him, I spun and fired shots in all different directions. I saw them move quickly, it even hit the side of one of the guards. Another guard was able to evade the fire and get past the firewall, before he was able to hit me, with what looked like an ax, I threw up a protection wall. His hit ricocheted back at him and flew him backwards.

Gary yelled out again, "Ouch, that must have hurt!" The crowd cheered.

I could see the guards through the flames and past them Ralph was being attacked by a guard. I quickly shot an air blade, the guards were able to dodge it, but it sliced at the guard that was attacking Ralph, cutting the guard's arm. He immediately backed off and moved to the wall. Ralph looked over and nodded but I was too late his egg had already been destroyed.

"I see she can be hot and spicy!" The crowd laughed at his comment. "But alas that is time!

I expelled the flame wall and Connor, and I were the only ones left. I looked back towards Gerard, but he was talking to the women, still not entertaining enough.

Gary spoke to the crowd again, "Everyone will go back to their cells and will take a quick break. Everyone can place their bids."

Everyone started heading back and I didn't see Lucia until I got back to the cell.

"Lucia! What happened?" She was holding onto her side. It was bleeding from a cut. Maybe a small airstrike.

"Don't worry it's nothing serious. Just makes me look bad." I couldn't heal it because then they would notice she had help.

"I'm sorry."

"Don't worry about it, nothing you could have done." She was right, I knew I couldn't help her, it made her look weak.

I got up and banged on the bars, "I want to speak to Lord Gerard!"

One of the guards came over, "You don't make commands here."

"Please, not a command, a request. One that I think he might find interesting." The guard snorted but left in the right direction.

It wasn't long before I felt him enter the cells. He was looking at us in a non-impressive gesture.

"You needed something?" He was standing with his arms crossed, I could see his biceps bulge, which I needed to refocus out of. His eyes though were dim, he was hungry, so he was cranky.

"I have a question, the other night you told me to play."

"Yes?"

"That whole thing was a setup wasn't it, with Galen and Kai. He was never in danger, you just wanted to test me?" He was smirking, now he was impressed. "Well, that was your turn, here's mine, buy Lucia."

He chuckled, "Why would I do that?"

"A gift for your nephew, she will get stronger, and if you do this, I will give you what you want." That piqued his interest.

"If it's good enough." He then turned and left for his seat. Damn, he has a nice ass, my god can I stop! I sighed in frustration.

"You didn't have to do that Ava." I turned back toward her.

"Yes, I did, I won't let you go to some sleazeball; besides, you and Galen get along, you would be good for him, help him grow up kind and strong." She smiled at the words, she hoped for the outcome.

CHAPTER FIVE

e were all brought out to the arena again. Gerard was speaking to Galen' mother, hopefully talking about his surprise for her son. I squeezed Lucia's hand and she squeezed back. Gary then came back out.

"Welcome back!" Everyone settled and quieted down again. "We've come to the final judgment, to see how strong they truly are. I hope you're ready ladies and gentlemen, I hope you haven't grown too attached to any one of them, in this round anything is possible." I watched him as he paced around in a circle, working the crowd up. "You see, for this round it is everyone for themselves, they will fight each other until one is standing. Now, we don't ask you to kill each other, just to the point of surrender; but be warned there have been some to lose limbs and even die."

The crowd cheered up in excitement, but I saw Galen go to his mom in protest. He genuinely cared for us, and that is something that all witches needed on their side.

"Now everyone spreads out and gets ready to begin."

"Lucia stayed with me, he never said we couldn't make alliances." She nodded and we moved away from the others. I saw a few other alliances form.

"And begin!"

I decided to break the ice this time. I put my hands on the ground and pulled up roots and grew tall trees into the arena.

"Holy shit, Ava!" I smiled, that's the first time I heard her swear. I looked at Gerard, I had his attention, even the women by his side were watching intently. It's been a while since I had a good challenge and could use a good amount of power. They would feel my aura from the stands, knowing now I could easily be a class five.

The roots would just slow others down, that way we couldn't be snuck upon. "Lucia I want you to project, be ready for anything that comes around." She nodded and went to sit on the ground.

"What do you see?"

"There are a couple of groups coming towards us." She looked up, "what are you going to do?"

I turned to her and smiled before I felt my skin give away, my body hunched, and I was on all fours, I had morphed into a black wolf with black eyes.

She stood up immediately, "Shadow work! That's dangerous Ava!" She came running at me, but I moved into the shadows before she could catch me.

I moved along the floor in the shadows of the trees. When I saw someone, I jumped out of the shadow and pounced on them. I snarled into his face, daring him to move.

"I surrender!" He screamed in a high-pitched voice. I got off him and let him run out of the arena. I heard a few others surrender from other battles.

I moved back into the shadow and was just about to go after someone else until I noticed it was Ralph. I moved out and back into my normal form.

"Well, aren't you one big surprise?" He spoke just like any old grandpa.

"Sorry, you know how dangerous these things can be."

"I know, something like this, I too would have hidden it. It must have been something important that made you come out of hiding." I nodded at him. "Well, then I know when I am beat, I surrender." He did a small bow to me and then headed out. I hoped that he would be safe in the future. He was a nice old man.

I heard a screeching scream knowing exactly who it was coming from. I moved back into the shadow. When I came back out in wolf form, Viera had a knife to Lucia's throat, and Connor was leaning on a tree waiting. I could see the cut on Lucia's arm. She was bleeding too much, she needed to be healed or she would die of blood loss."

I morphed back, "Let her go" I was mad, and boy they didn't want me to be mad.

They both threw back their heads in laughter. "Why the hell would we do that, we have the upper hand." Viera tugged on Lucia's hair exposing her neck more, pushing the knife harder, a small trickle of blood fell down her neck.

Connor pushed off the tree and came towards me, "this is how it's going to be; you're going to surrender to me, and I will come out victorious from this all."

I looked back towards Lucia, then back at him, "Connor have you ever had a nightmare that you would never wake up from?"

"Huh?"

I moved quickly and grabbed his arm, dragging him into the Shadow Realm. He wouldn't survive there; he would come out damaged. I left him there, for all the Shadows to torture him and make him go insane. When I came back out, Viera was pale.

"You bring him back." Her voice was broken.

"Let Lucia go first." She looked at Lucia then back at me. She pushed Lucia towards me, and I motioned for her to leave. Lucia left the arena holding her cut tight.

I went back into the Shadow Realm and found Connor floating, not moving. I pulled him out, he was unconscious. I got up and stood above him, Viera was by his side in an instant shaking him, trying to wake him up.

"People lose their minds if they're left there too long"

Everyone had access to the Shadow Realm if they could find it, just no one was dumb enough to risk it, for good reason.

"You ruined him!" She tried hitting me with an air blade but missed and just sliced a branch from a tree.

"I can bring him back." She looked at me desperately. "Just surrender, make this easy."

She looked confused but in a quiet voice, she surrendered. I smirked at her then kneeled next to Connor, I was very aware people were holding their breath in the stands. Even Gary didn't want to announce that I won right away.

I reached down past the ground into Connor's shadow, I pulled him closer until it was back where it was supposed to be. He opened his eyes screaming. Viera hugged him, crying. He held onto her, and she helped him up. They left the arena.

I looked over to where Gary was standing, then I spread out my arms and removed the trees and roots from the arena, forcing them back to the ground, so it was back to what it was before.

"Well, people I think we have seen something kind of a first here. I give you your winner Angelic!" People were cheering.

Looking up at Gerard, he was smirking with that hot half-smile he had and nodded in my direction. I decided to face the Royal family and bow. Then walked towards the gate out of the arena.

"Hold up" There were guards in front of me, I put my hands up hoping they knew I meant no harm. I turned back towards Gary. "You are quite powerful. I would think the crowd would feel safer if your powers were voided." I looked at him questioningly. He just turned back to Gerard.

Gerard just nodded, and then slid his fingers over the device.

"Gah!" I pulled at the device around my neck, I fell to one knee. "That really does fucking hurt." He then opened a small channel up minimal powers, but it was enough to void off the pain. He motioned for me to leave now. As I departed the guards moved aside, not wanting to get close.

In the cell, Lucia was getting healed by Gale. I just sat on the other bed watching. Truthfully, I was exhausted and needed to sleep, but I was too hyper-aware of everything going on around me. Some people were coming in looking at other witches, trying to decide if they wanted to buy them. A guard outside each cell would keep them at a distance but some people would try to press their faces to the bars.

I heard the guard unlock our cell and Galen came in with a small piece of paper in his hands. His mother was still standing at the door.

Galen's mother spoke up, "Gerard said you didn't disappoint; I, unfortunately, would have to agree." I only looked at her, Gerard gave me a compliment, she then turned to Gale, "How much longer Gale?"

"I would say she can travel now, my lady" Should have figured he was a capable healer being part of the Royal family.

Lucia stood up, gave a meek smile at me, and walked out of the cell. Only Galen and I remained in the cell, but the others were not far, especially Gale.

"That was quite the power you showed out there"

I smiled at him, "Was that a compliment? Or are you scared of me now too?" He reached out touching my hand.

"Something that powerful should be feared, but that's because they don't know you, you're loyal to those you care about. You protected me when I needed you." He looked over at Lucia. "I just don't think I would want to be your enemy."

I smiled at him, and tousled his hair, "Spoken like a true Royal."

"Come on Galen, let's go." His mother interjected.

"See you at home." He then ran off following his mother. The guard closed the gate and locked it back up. I doubt he would move far, but then again; I was probably too tired to really care either.

It was still full of hustle and bustle and a few gawkers. I decided to lay down, throwing my arm over my eyes. Damn, I needed a nap, but it was too noisy to sleep. I couldn't tell where Gerard was, or much of where anyone was.

After a while, it was starting to quiet down, and pretty much every other witch was gone. Maybe they were deciding if they wanted to kill me instead? Wouldn't be the first time they just killed strong witches. I heard footsteps down the hall, I sat up on the edge of the bed.

"You do realize what you have done, right?" He spoke almost as if he was angry.

"Honestly, I don't know. I can't figure out what the hell it is you want."

"I wanted to see strength, not your strongest spell so that everyone else could see and anticipate." He was angry, and hungry, a dangerous mix.

I smiled at him, "You think that was my strongest, that's sweet"

He studied me for a minute, "What are you?"

"I am a witch with skill and power." I stood up and walked up to the bars coming in close to Gerard. "But more importantly, I am incredibly dangerous."

"That could cost you your life." I just nodded at him, then returned to my seat. "How will I be able to trust you?"

"Can you trust the fact that I don't want to die?"

"If you're that strong, then why didn't you use it when we first met. You were free to use as much power as you wanted."

"Being hunted and killing everyone I come across isn't exactly a life I strive for. I had gone a long time traveling, never being found. I messed up and ran into the one being I tried very hard to avoid because I knew once I did, that be it, no more hiding." He seemed to accept my answer because he then pulled at the gate, and it broke open. He then started walking out of this shithole and I followed quickly behind him.

We came out of the stadium to the front where there were a few other carriages left. I saw Ralph, he nodded at me before disappearing into his own carriage. Gerard was talking to someone, and I was too tired to care what was happening, it does take a lot of power to create an entire forest and jump in and out of the Shadow Realm, apparently, he missed that part.

"Get in," he motioned for me to get into the carriage but when I went to take a step up, I missed but Gerard grabbed my arm quickly before I fell. His touch sent an electrical shock up my arm that made me shiver. I bet he felt it too, but he let me go and I forced myself up into the carriage. Gerard came in and sat on the opposite side staring, I couldn't tell if he thought I was a threat or just studying my movements. The carriage then pulled ahead and turned to stare out the window.

I was lulled to sleep by the quiet carriage ride. I dreamed of my mother, her telling me to hide in the Shadow Realm so they wouldn't find me. She promised that the shadow creatures won't hurt me. I had visited them often as a young child, they liked to play. I felt a shock wave above the ground. I knew it was her, my mother was dead, killing everyone close. I woke up in the dark carriage.

"Bad dreams?" He seemed genuinely concerned, a nice change.

"Just bad memories."

I looked out to see we were coming up to a huge gate, there was a giant mansion in the back, built with brick. It must be where his entire family lives. As we pulled into the gates, there were other houses around, probably for people like me and other workers. We were coming up to the main entrance when I sat back. Gerard had an amusing smug on his face.

"So, I've never seen any Royal home before, never wanted to get close enough."

"I can understand why." He then proceeded out of the carriage as one of the guards opened the door.

I followed behind him, and there seemed to be quite a few guards around. I hoped it was just for extra protection for the main entrance, but I doubted it.

"Your highness, Morgan requested your presence at the study hall." That must be the woman's name he was with.

"I'm sure, tell everyone to get back to their post, I think I can handle my own witch." I seemingly got goosebumps as he said, 'my own.' I do wonder how our fight would have been different if I went full out; but now was time to enter my new life, life at the Royal Palace, or just giant ass building.

CHAPTER SIX

The guard saluted and left to talk with the other guards, and Gerard continued into the mansion. Inside wasn't so bad. Little outdone with high ceilings, grand staircases, too many rooms, and weird paintings. I prefer a nice small home, with a good garden, and small creatures making homes in the flowers and trees.

"This way Angelic." He was already starting up the stairs and I had to run a bit to catch up. The sleep, or nightmare, in the carriage, wasn't enough for me to get back my energy and being mostly closed off from my magic with this thing around my neck is going to take me much longer.

I followed him a way, noticing a quaint library, and small business rooms. There were humans and vampires running around doing chores. He opened into a large room, it had a huge bed, large dressers, and closets. A study area next to a nice sitting window. Looking down I can see a quaint little home. Between the closet and study area was a door that seemed to be a bathroom. As I turned back around Gerard was standing there watching me analyze his bedroom... his bedroom, I think I blushed I didn't mean to, but this whole thing is new to me.

"I hope you enjoyed your tour, don't go anywhere." He headed towards the bathroom.

"Yes well, then I'll just stay over here." I stuttered out before he shut the bathroom door behind himself. That was embarrassing.

I sat by the window looking at the small home when I noticed Galen and Lucia heading inside. I wonder if that's where Lucia will stay? I need to talk to her, I need to make sure she understands, and that she doesn't hate me. I hadn't had a friend in so long I forgot how they worked. I looked back towards the bathroom, there was no way I would chance leaving and getting back before he was done. Just then I heard the shower turn off.

He came out with pants on but no shirt. His broad shoulders and defined abdomen were too much, I couldn't process him right now, too much else was in my head. I turned to look out the window and saw Galen leave. I will have to get down there. Then someone knocked on the door. I turned with Gerard fully dressed.

"Morgan," he left the door open and walked away from it to sit in his chair at his study.

"I didn't think you would have company, isn't it a little dangerous to be alone with her." She gazed an ugly look at me.

"That's not your concern. What do you want?"

"I told your guard to tell you we need you in the meeting room, we need to go over some certain plans with you." She was obviously trying to avoid giving off too much information while I was here.

"Very well, Angelic you stay here." He was starting to head out with her.

"Wait, do you think I can go see Lucia; I saw her go into the house there." I pointed out towards the window, but he knew which place I meant.

"They won't trust you to go around the castle on your own. Just stay here for now." He then left, shutting the door, and ending any protests I may have.

I looked back out the window and noticed she was still in there. I rummaged through Gerard' desk and found paper and pencils.

Lucia,

Please forgive me for what I did. I didn't mean to keep it a secret but It's dangerous for people when they know my true powers. I don't want to be in this awkward place with you. If you can accept my apology, please come out of the house and wave towards the mansion. You will see me at the window.

-Angelic

I folded the paper, giving it wings. I opened the window and let it fly out into the air. It flew down and slowly made its way to the home. It flew right at her window. She opened it up and grabbed it. Now I just have to hope that she comes out. After a few sweaty minutes, she came out and looked over. I waved down at her, and she waved back with a smile. Thank you, I tried telling her, she nodded at me and then went back inside.

I retreated into the room, I was starving and tired. I decided to lay down at the end of the bed. Using it normally would just feel too weird. It didn't take me long to fall asleep, thankfully I had a dreamless sleep.

I was shaking, "Angelic woke up, it's nearly supper time." I woke up to Galen shaking my shoulder.

I rubbed my eyes as I stood up. "I'm sorry, what did you say Galen?"

"They want you down to eat supper with all of us."

"Okay just give me a moment." I sleepily pulled myself off the bed and made my way into his bathroom.

The bathroom was larger than most of the rooms I had stayed in. There were two sinks, a soaker tub, and a stand-up shower. As I turned to look at the golden trim mirror, I saw myself, my hair was rattled and matted. I was able to use a bit of magic and clean it up and wave it out around myself, it was quite long from over the years only hiding and running. I figured I was good enough and came back out to Galen patiently waiting by the bed.

"Thanks for waiting," I smiled at him.

"No problem!" He then proceeded out the door and I followed in pursuit.

The hallways were not as crowded but there were a few people loitering around. They obviously avoided us. One person even went back down the stairs as we were coming down.

Coming into the dining area, it was a long grand table, with servants around. The table had normal-looking food, but the red bowl and glasses of red liquid was obvious. Sometimes it's easy to forget what they are.

Galen took his seat next to Lucia, and I took a seat next to the head of the table where Gerard was sitting. That woman Morgan was on the other side, Galen' mother was at the other end, I was sitting next to Gale.

"I'm sure you must be hungry Angelic," Gale stated to me with a friendly greeting. Kind of nice compared to the ice-cold stares as of late.

"I am very much." I heard a snort come from Morgan. What is her issue? I liked to push buttons though, "I wonder if some think I'm just too powerful to even be here, maybe we're matching their own strengths." Galen knew my reference and giggled. Morgan ignored my remarks. Gerard though gave me a correction glare. I just moved on to eating my food.

After a bit of silence Galen spoke up, "I think it will be interesting to see Gale and Angelic fight." Gale and I both choked on whatever we were eating at that moment. We kind of looked at each other and laughed.

"Galen, I don't think you understand, what she did today puts her at a much higher level than even me, maybe even more than anyone around." Gale tried to explain to Galen, but he didn't seem to get it.

I spoke up then, "I don't think anyone around trusts me enough to fight anyone right now."

"But why? Because you can go to the Shadow Realm?"

"Partly, but also because I became one with the Shadows, I

transformed into a black wolf, that's power from the shadow realm and dangerous to use if the Shadow King doesn't approve." His eyes seemed to enlarge.

He yelled out in excitement, "Yeah! That was awesome!" I shook my head and held in my laughter; he was too cute but naive.

"I'll fight her." I looked over at Gerard. He was serious and didn't falter in his dare.

"I'm supposed to protect you, not hurt you."

"What makes you think you can hurt me?" I didn't have a response; I didn't really know for sure. He is older, and royalty. He has strength and healing beyond my own comprehension.

Galen spoke up, killing the awkward stare Gerard and I were sharing, "I think that would be awesome to see, she's so strong and I've never seen Uncle Gerard lose to anyone."

"I think if that is what he wants, then I'll accept. It'll help me understand what you will need from me in future battles." He took his glass and tilted it at me before taking a drink. I think he agreed in both ways.

"Are you well enough for a fight now?"

Of course, he wanted to do this now, he doesn't seem like a patient man when there is something he wants. Looking at my plate, "Yes I can battle now. Am I getting all my power back?"

"Of course," He was grinning, and it didn't seem innocent.

We all finished up our food and cleared out of the dining area and headed out to the courtyard. By this time, it was dark out and there were a lot of stars, the waxing moon was glowing. It was refreshing to see. This was going to be a spectator show, and everyone was going to watch.

I made my way out to one end and Gerard went to the other. He pulled out the device and once he swiped over it, I felt my powers return. It felt almost unreal, I sparked some electricity in my fingers just to make sure.

"Are you ready?"

I looked over at our crowd. Morgan was closer to Gerard, I

wonder if she was jealous right now? I nodded at him. In that second, he was gone out of my sight.

I immediately put up an invisible maze. He was only a few feet away when he stopped in front of a wall.

He tapped on the wall, "not bad." Then he was gone again, going through the maze, almost like he could see the walls.

I had to move fast, I knew he wanted me to use it, it was too obvious, but I was curious as to why. Luckily, it's dark outside and easy to fall into the darkness of the shadow. I moved quickly before he reached me. I dived into the shadow and moved across the field in a matter of seconds. I had to release the walls because they served no purpose besides diminishing my power and focus.

He searched for me, but he found me in moments. No one can find me in the shadows, he's different unless this is just what a truly powerful Vampire can do. I stayed where I was and as soon as he was close enough, I pounced on him in my wolf form. I was heavy enough to throw him off balance and make him fall into the Realm.

I didn't force us further than I needed, I didn't want to put him in any real danger. He grabbed my paw and threw me away from him, but he didn't move from there. He was looking around, analyzing this place.

"Why did you want to come here, and why didn't you just ask?" I was back in my regular form when his eyes settled on me.

"I have read about it before. I wanted to see it for myself." He started to look around again.

I crossed my arms, "And my second question?"

He smiled, "As you said, you need to know if you're capable of protecting me if we get into battle."

"And your verdict?"

"You would be an adequate partner in battle." He really wasn't paying much attention to me. It was almost like he had life back in his eyes, finding a new discovery. I liked that I got to bring him that.

"We have to go back, if we linger too long the Shadow Creatures will find us and drag you down, and I'm not sure if I could stop them."

He agreed with me, and I pulled us out of the shadows and back into the night. I laid on my back breathing harder than I should have been. Passing two people through the realms seemed to take a lot out of me.

"I think you need to stop cutting my powers off." He glanced down at me, I sat up looking at him, "It's taking me too long to recover from the cut-offs, I'm not healing fast enough, and when you need me, I might not be helpful." I was still trying to catch my breath between sentences.

"I can see that but trust me if you betray me even once I will cut you off and won't give them back." He then walked to Morgan, and they walked back into the Manor together.

Watching them go was disappointing, as much as I try to tell myself they're not lovers, it was starting to become too obvious. I felt someone hug me from behind pulling me from my dangerous thoughts.

"Hey Galen, have you learned anything from the fight?" He came around to sit in front of me.

"Definitely! My uncle is super strong but you're the first to ever catch him in a spell!" I didn't have the heart to tell him he did that on purpose.

"Thanks, Galen, now why don't you go back inside with your mother."

"Okay, I'll see you two tomorrow." He ran back to his mother holding her hand, giving her back a play-by-play of the fight that she had already witnessed herself.

Lucia and I were the only ones remaining, along with the guards that never went too far.

"Hey," she said

"Hey," I stood up standing next to her, "Lucia I am sorry about what happened, I'm not used to having other people around, or friends."

"It's fine, really, come on, let's go back to our home."

"Our home?"

"Gerard didn't tell you? They gave us a small house on the East end. It's close enough if they need us and we can continue studying, and you can continue training me." She had a big grin on her face.

I hugged her; I haven't had someone like her in my life since I was a child. Running my whole life, avoiding being caught. It was constantly like a nightmare. Life is full of funny little surprises. With our arms wrapping around each other's shoulders, we stumbled over each others' feet heading towards our new home.

It was a small home with an open space, a small bathroom and one bedroom but enough room for two beds and two dressers. I had no complaints. Over the season, we filled it with flowers and life. We had our own small garden that no one seemed to mind. Galen enjoyed learning everything, and Lucia was becoming a strong advanced level 2. I had put her at level three, but she refused to believe it.

"Can you just agree with me, then we can move on to more complex spells." I was sitting by the window, the one facing Gerard' room. I had only heard from him maybe a handful of times. I had heard he, and Morgan were planning a trip in the coming Holiday.

Lucia sat beside me handing me a steamy cup of tea that smelled of jasmine. "If I do agree, can you promise me not to go overboard? It still scares me to think that I advanced so quickly."

"Maybe your teacher was just talented." I winked at her. "Listen, I'll go to the library for some aid on teaching level three spells. I don't want you to get hurt by doing something too strong either, I know how you like to not say 'no'." I turned to look out the window just in time to see Morgan at his window, and like the beady-eyed woman she is, she turned to see me. I instantly turned back to Lucia who was going on about the safety of spell casting.

I put my drink down, "It will be fine Lucia." I got up and grabbed my cloak, it looked like we would have snow soon.

"Fine but be careful. I have to go to town with Galen and Gale today. He wants to find a present for his mother for the upcoming Holiday."

"Perfect, that'll give me plenty of time to put something together for us. I'll see you tonight."

We waved goodbye and I was out fast-paced walking to the library. I stopped for a moment to watch my breath. I breathed out and it snowed and fell gently to the ground. I loved simple magic more than the big stuff. Not paying attention I had almost run into the trunk of a tree, looking up it was beautifully grown, with strong limbs. Going close I could tell he had seen this place when it was nothing more than a forest. I felt a chill down my spine and decided to rush inside.

I was busy with the start of the new day. Everyone was rushing for breakfast or to get a head start on chores. They would be having people come from across the land to celebrate another year and to prepare for the upcoming Winter.

When I got to the top of the stairs, I saw Gerard and Morgan together in the hall. She had him pressed against the wall trying to stop him from going anywhere. She grabbed his shirt and brought him down to kiss her.

I really didn't mean for it to happen but seeing it pissed me off. I clenched my hands to try and stop it, but it was too late. The force was out and the painting just to the right of them came crashing down. It made them pull apart and look for the culprit, obviously with my talents I was already gone. I was in the library before anyone suspected me.

It was small and musty. The smell of old books and their stories spilling out from every corner. A few seats and a couch with red velvet covers seemed to fit the library well, and the two long windows let in just enough light. Going over a few sections I found a few books that looked promising, deciding to sit at the long couch facing the window before diving deep into them.

I was too focused on my reading to notice when someone entered the library and sat beside me, but I did not have to look at him to know who it was.

"That was an original painting I hope you know," Gerard said

I looked over at him, "I wouldn't know what you're talking about."

"Either way, try to contain your powers, or I will have to turn that back on." He touched the collar on my neck. His fingers lingering only for a moment, and I knew he could feel my pulse quicken at his touch.

"Have you ever had witches' blood?" It kind of stumbled out but he seemed interested in the question.

"Once, it was quite painful, I wasn't as strong as I am today though."

"Do you think mine would hurt you?"

He did that half-smile that I love, "Why? Did you want to try?"

"Whoa, I'm pretty sure you would have a harder time than I would."

He reached over to pull my hair back, "Why don't we find out," he was leaning in so close I could smell his cologne, it was sweet-smelling with a bit of musk. His lips were at my neck. I moved my arm to grab the top of the couch, the book in my other hand fell to the ground. He had small hairs that tickled my neck causing an electrical outburst.

He pulled back just in time before Morgan walked in, "Gerard we have to go, people will be coming soon, and we have to be prepared with the humans."

He reluctantly got up, taking his time, almost like he was disappointed. If he was willing to take the witch's blood, he would probably be very hungry.

"Gerard," he turned back towards me, "Try to get something to eat, you'll only put yourself in danger and I'll have to come save your ass." He smiled.

"Have a good day Angelic."

They had both left and I was in a kind of haze. What was I thinking? My magic in his body could have killed him! I needed to start practicing my impulses around him. For both our sakes.

I took the books back with me to our house. It is, by far, safer to be in my own dwelling than somewhere I could do something dangerously impulsive again.

I came up with some great ideas before Lucia got home. She didn't say much before going to bed which seemed odd for her, Galen must have tired her out. I decided it was getting late and it would be a good idea to get some sleep too. Tomorrow we would have to be on our best behavior for our guests.

CHAPTER SEVEN

Lucia was gone by the time I got up, which was a little disappointing, I was really excited to tell her she will finally be learning some fire skills. The house was filled with the glow of the morning sun, and the snow was glazed over the fields outside reflecting the light to create a beautiful morning glow. Shortly after starting a fire and putting the kettle on there was a knock at the door.

"Good morning, Galen."

"Ava! I was hoping you were still here. Lucia said she couldn't wake you, that you were sleeping like the dead."

"Oh, that's odd, usually I wake up pretty easily." Must be getting a little too comfortable being here.

"That's ok but we're all having breakfast together. Though just be prepared there will be other vampires and witches at the table."

"I see, alright then why don't you go ahead and tell them I'll be there shortly." Galen nodded then ran off.

This wasn't going to be the typical breakfast; something was going to be amiss. I did up my long hair into a nice bun, then put on the nicest pants and shirt I had. I did not want to embarrass Gerard with my lack of wardrobe. Heading out and trudging through the snow I made it inside. There were guards placed at all entrances and people were running and yelling getting ready for the Gala tonight.

Coming around the corner hoping to not be late I ran into something knocking me back. Someone had caught my arm before I fell completely back onto my butt. Looking back up I saw beautiful blue eyes and a stunning smile. Quickly I yanked my hand back.

"I am so sorry; I wasn't paying attention and I came around the corner too fast."

"Don't worry about it. The name Marcus." He did a slight bow. He had sandy brown hair, and was quite tall, maybe as tall as Gerard but I doubt it.

"Hello, I am Angelic." I copied his bow.

"Well seeing as I am new here and completely lost, could you tell me where to get to the Royal dining area?" He had a very charming voice with an accent that placed him from out of town.

"Oh, of course, that is actually where I am heading so we can just go together." I continued down the hallway and he followed beside me. "So, you're a mage then, right?"

"I am."

"Did you come from out of town with another Noble family?"

"I came with my Master." He had a stern face saying that. He must not be all too pleased with whoever his master is.

"I see."

We came up to the door to the dining area rather quickly and I could hear people yelling and laughing.

"I suppose we should go in." He smiled back at me and opened the door.

Walking in the smell hit me first then the sight of eggs, meat, and fruit were displayed over the table. There were at least three new faces I didn't recognize. I took my seat next to Gerard and Gale. Marcus sat next to the two new Vampires, then there was a small boy talking with Galen.

"Gerard, this must be your new witch."

"She is my very late witch, yes." I just turned away.

"Ah well, Marcus here was late too."

Gerard turned to me, "And why were you late together?"

"We just kind of met in the hallway, he was lost and needed directions."

"I see, well Angelic this is my brother Adam, his wife Laura, and their son Cade."

"It is a pleasure meeting you all." I bowed my head.

I looked over at Lucia and noticed she was giving Marcus the once over. I decided to fill up my plate as a way to avoid conversation. They all went on about the events tonight, they seemed worried the humans wouldn't be able to handle everything in time.

"Ava!" Galen yelled across the table.

startled, I looked over at Galen, "Yes, Galen."

"Can you read Marcus? I told Cade you can pretty much tell the strength of any witch and vampire."

"I don't think that would be a good idea." I looked over at Gerard who never objected. "Alright then."

Looking over at Marcus, he was smiling. He had an extraordinarily strong aura in him. "Well from what I can tell he is definitely a class five, and if he hasn't realized that yet, then he has the capabilities of being one.

"Thank you, Angelic, I am indeed a class five, but I too am skilled in reading witches. For example, Lucia here is easily a class three."

"See! I keep telling her this, but she does not listen." He laughed.

"It is scary going up to a new level when one is not ready, but I would assume you would know nothing of that?" The table went silent, and I could feel Gerard staring at me.

"And what do you mean by that Marcus?" I asked.

"Your aura is very dark; it is like a bottomless pit. One goes too far and they could go mad in the darkness. This either tells me you're not all witch, or you uncovered a power that no one else has."

"I think that would be enough," Gerard spoke.

"Of course, Lord Gerard." Markus gave him a bow and continued with his food.

Everyone was finishing up and the boys wanted to go outside, Lucia would keep an eye on them, which means no training. I wanted to talk to Marcus more, but a hand latched onto my arm and started dragging me out of the room. Gerard was leading me back to his room, surely to try and understand what exactly Marcus meant.

Once inside he pushed me to his chair and forced me to sit, then went back and slammed the door. He was mad. I could feel his anger radiate off him, unfortunately, with vampires they can be pretty unstable sometimes.

"Tell me what you are now."

"I am a witch. I was born from a witch." Gerard sighed and ran his fingers through his hair. He wasn't sure what to do with me, whether I needed to be killed or not. "Gerard, I do not want to die. I can promise you that I will not hurt anyone unless you ask me to, like you said I am *your* witch."

"You're one of them, the stronger ones, the ones that can kill this entire household. If that is the case, then you should be sentenced to death." I couldn't move, I didn't want to die, and I always knew if I was found this would be my undoing, if I even flinched he would snap my neck before I could even let out one spell.

"I am strong, I can do things others can not, but how many times do I have to tell you my loyalty is to you, that I do not want to be on the run anymore. I have a home, a friend , a life that I could actually get used to."

His arms were crossed staring at me. "You're only loyal to me then?"

"Yes."

"And you'll do what I ask?"

"Whatever you need."

"Alright then, follow me." Gerard got up and started heading out the door. I'm not sure what he had in mind but whatever he asked, I would have to do it, otherwise, he will probably just kill me.

He walked at a fast pace, causing me to practically jog behind him. Everyone that we passed would either bow their head or try to speak to him. He only kept moving forward. We were about to head downstairs when she showed up.

"Gerard, what are you doing? We have guests to entertain unless you are planning on throwing her in the dungeons for lying about who or what she is, whatever that may be." Morgan said.

"What I have planned is none of your concern. Go handle the guests on your own for now I will be back shortly." Gerard then continued past her and I followed. She had crossed her arms and stared at me like I was an annoying fly.

We continued down the stairs, then through another hallway until we reached a door. Gerard pulled out some keys and unlocked it, then continued. It was a darker place, cold, wet, and we truly were heading to the dungeon, personally, I didn't think this place had one.

We go to a row of cells, ones a lot like where I was at the stadium. Luckily most were empty, and no witches were down here but there was one vampire. We stopped in front of his cell and he looked ragged. Crouched on the stone floor in the corner he had his face in his arms. He never looked up even when Gerard opened the door.

"Angelic met Liam, he had been following Galen the other day. Lucia had pointed it out while they were in town."

"Lucia has been training a lot to focus on who is around her."

"Yes, and it is good training to have. She started to teach Gale how to do this as well." He turned fully towards me, "I need you to get him to tell us why. Pain has been deemed useless and Gale couldn't make him snap. Now it's your turn." He was studying me, waiting for me to reject.

"As you wish."

Walking towards this guy made a lot of memories come back. The things I have done to get out of trouble are far from innocent, but I would need to do this. Kneeling on the stone floor I touched his knee. His head shot up staring at me with one eye, he still had the blood on his face from the other one they pulled out. If he can handle that then it will take a lot more than a few scorch marks to get him to talk.

"And what is this one going to do, burn me? Drown me? Maybe suffocation." These were all true technically. Gerard just stood there with his arms crossed and he gestured to me to continue.

"You seem to have a pleasure for torture."

"Don't speak to me you filthy witch, I am a vampire you bow to me!" I slapped him across the face.

"It really pisses me off when you all think that, maybe your King there has power over me, but you do not. You are nothing and unless you tell me why you were following Master Galen, I will unleash a lot of my hate onto you."

He leaned back and spat at me. It hit my barrier around me and fell to the floor, and with a snap of my fingers, his mouth was sealed shut. Watching his eyes bulge from his head, desperately scratching at his face was amusing, Gale must have gone easy on him. Releasing his hold, I let him speak.

"What the hell! Witches can't do that!"

"If that is what you think then you know very little of what we can really do." The man's head leaned back raising his arms to push me away but I placed my hand on his head first. He stopped moving instantly and was frozen. I dragged him down into his own mind causing a type of dream state for him, but unfortunately for him, he will feel everything.

"Where am I?"

"We're inside your head, of course, I can't see any of your

memories otherwise that will be too easy. What I can do though is create eternal suffering."

I used an airstrike to create a laceration across his belly. He immediately fell to the floor screaming in pain.

"The thing about this place is you lose all your vampire abilities, no more fast healing, no more numbing the pain. You will feel everything and heal just as I want you to."

Watching him roll around on the pitch-black floor wasn't going to be enough, and I knew what I needed to do but I could hear my mother asking me not to. She always warned me not to go too far into the Shadows, otherwise, He would find me. I looked back at Gerard, he never moved, he couldn't see what was happening, but he wasn't going to tell me to stop.

"Tell me why you were following them."

"Fuck you witch!"

"Listen this is going to get a whole lot worse before it gets better, just tell me."

He just stared at me, daring me to burn him or drown him, but unfortunately for him, I had worse nightmares.

"Suit yourself."

I started to create a few rats, too many would be too quick but with a few, it would be very slow. They started to run towards him, the black fur made them blend into the ground. He didn't have a chance to get away from them. He screamed as they borrowed themselves into his open abdomen. Eating the warmth of his intestines. He would never die since this wasn't his real body, but he would lose a bit of his mind the longer he let this continue.

I knelt close to his face, "If you don't tell me now, I will never make it stop and this will repeat over and over again." I got back up and stepped away.

He continued to holler and scream but it didn't take long before he screamed out.

"Morgan! Ok, it was Morgan!" I immediately pulled away

and we were back in his cell. He leaned over to the side and vomited what little was in his guts.

I got up and turned back to Gerard, "You hear that?"

"I did." He then proceeded down to the man grabbing his hair and slamming him against the wall. Now it was my turn to watch him work. "Tell me what she wanted you to do?"

He was silent but he looked at me then immediately answered him, "She wanted me to tell her everything that he was doing. Where he was going, what people he talked to. What shops he went to."

"Why?" Gerard' voice was very deep, he was threatening him, and it even sent chills down my spine.

"She never said why, she just paid me and told me to never speak of it to anyone not even if it caused my death, but she never mentioned an eternity of that!" He pointed towards me.

"Because she doesn't know, and no one ever will." Gerard placed both his hands on him and snapped his neck.

He did a long sigh before turning back to me, "You will not do that ever again unless I ask you to. I have seen what witches can do for torture but never that."

"It is a unique skill." I was tired though, my eyes felt heavy.

He reached his hand out and brushed some of my hair back. "Go home, you will need to rest before the party, and I do expect you to be there."

"Really, can't I just skip this one? Parties aren't really something I am good at."

"Whatever I say, remember."

I just rolled my eyes. "Yes."

"Good, now go."

I walked out without him. He probably needed to take care of the body then return to his guests. Though I wonder if he will confront Morgan first.

CHAPTER EIGHT

Walking up to my door I could hear the kettle going off. Lucia was in and I'm sure I carried an expression of loss. It takes a lot out of me to turn someone's mind inside out; but it also takes a lot of my own mind to do it. I just needed to rest then everything would be right as rain.

Walking in though Lucia saw my expression and immediately stopped what she was doing.

"What happened to you?"

"I don't think right now is a good time to talk about it." I tried sneaking past her, but she blocked my way.

"No, you sit and talk about it now."

"Lucia even if I wanted to I can't. This was something asked of me by Gerard and I don't think sharing this experience is something I'm allowed to share."

"He didn't..." She put her hands to her face, and I knew exactly what she was asking.

"No, he did not, now I am going to go into our room and sleep before the whole charade of tonight starts."

She moved aside and let me move past her. I shut the door behind me, I didn't want to be disturbed and wanted to sleep as much as I could before I had to entertain his guests. It didn't take me long to fall asleep after hitting my pillow.

There was a small chill in the air, and I knew the fire was out and Lucia had already gone. Opening the door there was a note on the table and a dress draped over the chair.

Do not be late, I doubt Gerard will be too happy if you were. I put your dress out, I figured these things are something you're not overly knowledgeable about, so Galen and I picked one out for you.

See you soon,

Lucia

Lifting the gown, it would be a full-length dress with an open back and long sleeves. It was as black as charcoal and would suit me just fine. I decided to put my hair up in a bun with a few curled pieces loose. The shoes were simple basic black heels. The only problem with all of this was having to walk across the snowy courtyard. I decided to wear my normal shoes until I got across and into the manor.

Coming up to the ballroom I could hear the sound of a piano playing with violins and cellos. I quickly switched my footwear and took off my shawl and gave them to one of the workers. Walking into a room filled with vampire royals and nobles made my skin crawl. The amount of power energized in this room felt like it could explode.

"She finally arrives."

I turned around to see Marcus in a beautiful black tux but if I looked in the light the right way you could see a hint of blue, he had it paired with a white shirt and black tie. "Marcus." I nodded my head at him. He ended up closing the gap between us by wrapping his arm around my waist and grabbing my other hand and placing it on his shoulder. "What are you doing?"

"You may be more powerful, but I doubt you can dance." He started to lead me out onto the dance floor with such soft move-ments you would almost think he was a vampire. "Be sure to look at me and not at your feet, otherwise you'll trip."

"Sorry, definitely not a dancer." I looked up into his blue eyes, immediately my mind went to the vampire in the cellar missing one of his. It caused me to look away and trip over his feet. He immediately corrected us, and we fluently continued with the dance.

"Something startled you, what was it?"

"It was nothing." There was no way I could let anyone know what happened. "Tell me Marcus, do you enjoy working for Gerard' brother?"

"Of course, I sought him out. I showed a lot of promise as a child and I wanted to practice and become as powerful as I could." So, he was one of those. "You're not impressed."

"No, it's not that."

"You have a different power and want to hide it. Why are you scared of it?" I saw Gerard over in the corner with Elanor and his brother and his brother's wife. They were fully engaged in their conversation except for Gerard who was staring straight at me.

"I'm sorry Marcus but there is nothing to be discussed on this subject. I am a witch, born and bred." The music came to an end and he let me go.

"Well then Angelic, until next time." He gave me a slight bow before departing and heading towards Gerard and his family.

It was truly beautiful here, there was a lot of deep navy blue with sparkling silver giving off a night-time sky look. There were a lot of tables set up with different vendors, and of course a red flowing fountain. I don't believe it was blood because that much blood would have a pretty bad smell, red wine I believe is what they were serving. I felt an arm loop around mine, looking over was a spectacular looking Lucia.

"Lucia that dress!" It was well silhouetted around her petite frame with sparkling silver and a deep V-neck.

"Never mind me, look at you! I knew I was right and that it would be perfect for you. You probably feel even too exposed with the open back."

"No, it's great, thank you."

"Well come on there is some amazing food here that you have to try."

She pulled me along through the crowd landing us in front of a long table full of different food. Some small sandwiches, cheese, crackers, small desserts. She was right most of the time I spent eating stale bread and anything I could get my hands on. She handed me a plate and we started diving in, adding whatever we could. We were then able to find some free seats with Galen and Cade.

"I saw you dancing with that Marcus guy, do you like him?" Galen asked.

"You really like to just jump right into the questions don't you."

"Cade said if you two got married you would have to leave us." Galen looked physically sad, to think he would even believe that, it hurt.

"No, I would never leave here unless asked to by your uncle. Marcus just wanted a partner to dance with." Galen smiled up at me then punched Cade in the arm.

"My father told me that he could get you two together if he wanted too" He spoke in the same accent as they all had, and the child made me want to seriously worry about his upbringing. He will probably look down on almost everyone but his family.

"I am sorry Cade but that won't happen, I would rather die." I was not going to sugar coat it to this kid. He did not deserve my respect.

"Well I think this conversation should come to an end. Galen, did you give your mother your gift?" Lucia spoke to Galen. Diverting anymore of that last conversation away.

"No, but I need to go to my room first to grab it."

"Why don't I come with you, it will be safer."

"I'm coming too, this party is too stuffy." They all started to get up.

"Are you coming Ava?" Lucia asked.

"No, you guys go and have fun, I'll wait here."

They said their goodbyes and departed out of the ballroom. The kid was definitely right, it was very stuffy in here. There were vampires flirting with each other, some even trying to prey on the humans for food. I even saw one leave with one. My food was increasingly appealing, and I just wanted to leave, the thought of even having to be here to entertain was miserable. I enjoyed my solitude and would much rather be there reading.

"You could come stand by my side if it makes you more comfortable." I looked up to see Gerard.

"I think more people would just stare at me then." He then sat down beside me. I looked over to see Morgan talking to his brother and Marcus. She was, though, giving quick glances over.

"I don't think Morgan is very comfortable with you by my side and not by hers." He gave me a confused look, making him look very cute. I had to turn away before I blushed looking at him.

"Ava, stop trying to hide it, it had been obvious since the day I saw you."

"I have no idea what you're talking about." I gave him the biggest smirk I could. There was no way I was admitting I was attracted to him.

"Of course you don't." He just returned a smirk that did make me blush while looking at him.

This moment came to a quick end when we heard someone scream. Gerard was gone in a second, I on the other hand needed a moment to even find where it was coming from. It had come from Galen' mother who was standing over top of his pale, unconscious body. I quickly ran up next to Lucia.

"What happened!" Gerard addressed the room, but it was Morgan that answered.

"We're not sure, he was talking to Cade and then all of a sudden he collapsed."

Gerard was in front of Lucia for a second, "You're supposed to protect him from what happened!"

"I'm not sure, he was fine, he hasn't shown any signs of being ill. We had just run back to get his room to grab his mother's gift and when we came back into the ballroom, he said he felt dizzy then collapsed."

"It is true my Lord, he has done nothing that would suggest being ill," Gale said, coming out of the crowd.

I walked past Gerard and he let me go to Galen freely. I knelt beside Galen and Gale followed, "What do you think Angelic?"

"I think I know but I just don't see how it could be possible." This looked all too familiar, and not in a good way.

"Tell me Angelic, what is wrong with my son!"

"I think it's a desert parasite, but Galen wouldn't have been anywhere near the desert and there is no way they could survive in our climate. This would have to be deliberate if it is this parasite."

"My Lord I can not remove it if it is what she says, these creatures dwell inside the body feasting on blood until there is no more. They are very small but grow in size and by the time it grows large enough for me to be able to move it, it would be too late. The parasite will essentially cause him to starve to death." Gale explained.

"Ava can, I'm sure of it," Lucia said

"Lucia it's not that easy, if I lose focus even slightly, I could permanently damage something."

Gerard kneeled beside me, "Do what you can, I will protect you if someone tries to get too close." I felt a warmth in his words. No one has ever promised my protection, not since my mother.

I leaned over Galen and placed both hands over top of him, I had to find the little shit first. It's not easy finding such a small creature in a body though. I moved my hands over top of each other, then I thought of something. I focused on the air and dropped the temperature to even colder than a vampire's temperature. This was excruciatingly cold for me, but it was bearable for a short period of time.

"Stop her! She's going to hurt him." Morgan yelled but

Gerard stopped her coming at me and I continued what I was doing.

The cold will slow it down and hopefully enough that I could find it. Searching along I finally found an abnormal feeling in Galen' body, here it was, now I really needed to focus. I had to force it out, but if I used too much it could burst out of his body.

Slowly but surely it started to move. I pushed it along until it reached his hand, I lifted it and created a small cut. Now I could levitate the thing out. It was a long one, but I think I was able to get it before it caused too much damage. Once it was completely out, I was looking at it while it squirmed around in its hold. I didn't care much for killing creatures, but this thing was going to burn. It turned to ash starting at both ends and meeting in the middle.

I stepped back away from Galen, "He needs blood, lots of it."

Everyone was crowding him in seconds, and I had to stand up and back out of the crowd before I passed out. Galen's mother grabbed her son and headed out of the ballroom. A few others followed but Gerard stayed and was just staring at me. I pulled back and walked out of this place before I started seeing stars.

Once I was back, I crashed right on my bed, not even bothering to take off my dress. Cuddling up to my pillow, earlier events were still weighing heavy on my mind, and I can only hope he won't find me, but before I could get too deep into my thoughts everything went black and I fell into a deathly sleep.

The fire was burning when I woke up and it was dark. I must have slept the whole day. This dress was tangled all of the way around me and had to come off immediately. Changing into something more comfortable, I went to make tea.

Sitting at our table looking into the dark sky, it seemed very quiet. I couldn't even detect a whole lot of guards out there. I searched for Gerard but couldn't find him, nor his sister, or brother. I did, however, found Galen. I immediately got up and ran to him. There weren't many inside, a few humans, some vampires, but no one I even recognized.

Probably be best to avoid all contact. I pulled myself into the shadows until I reached Galen' room. Hiding in the shadow I noticed there was a vampire guard in front of his door, one I did not recognize. I snuck inside, Galen was crouched on his bed, holding onto his pillow. His cousin was sitting beside him. Then there were two vampires guarding the inside of the door.

I came out of the shadows, before they could notice I electrified them, they fell to the ground steam coming off their now chard bodies. The guard outside stormed through the door, hitting my back, it startled me long enough for him to grab my throat. Big mistake on his part. I placed my hands on his arm and burned him, it traveled up his arm and burned him from the inside out. He could barely let out a squeal before he was dead.

"Ava!" He ran at me and gave me a huge hug. Cade was hesitant but I sat on the side of the bed and he came over and hugged me too. They were both very scared.

I pulled back from them, "Tell me what is going on?"

Galen spoke first, "It was Morgan, she drugged Gerard during the confusion. Then all these guards came marching into the castle."

"There from the dessert," Cade finished.

"That explains the parasite." Galen nodded; he still looked a bit pale but better than what he was.

"Do you know where they were taken?"

They both shook their heads. I can find them, but it will take a lot to move that quickly in the Shadow Realm.

"Alright, you two stay here. I will charge the outside of the door so no one will enter."

"I want to go with you." Galen was trying to look so strong but he would only be in the way.

"Galen, you will have to trust me I will save your uncle," I turned to Cade, "And your father." They both gave me another hug.

"Be safe, and don't die."

I laughed, "Me die? Never." I smiled down at them, then placed my hands on the door. It flared with blue light then looked like a normal door again. Turning to them I winked, then walked into the wall molding into the shadow. They would see a black figure rush through the walls before disappearing.

This world was always tricky to navigate, it feels like you're swimming but really, you're just floating around in the darkness. The closer you are to the surface you get more light but the deeper you go the darker it gets, and that's where most of the creatures live.

I moved quickly out of the manor to the courtyard, I moved to the town but still no sign of him. I moved out to the forest, but it wasn't right. This is going to be impossible, but then I felt someone, they were reaching for me. It was Lucia, I felt quite a bit of pride that she's grown so much that her message has reached me.

It didn't take me long to figure out where it was coming from, and I hated where it made me end up in the trials stadium. I came out of the shadow in the stands. Everyone missing was here, and Gerard was there in the middle, chained like an animal bleeding and the one holding the knife was Morgan. I probably enjoyed this fact more than I should have, mostly because she's fair game now.

I had another issue though, the other people, guards, and vampires here were from the desert lands. I had to get closer, getting down to the middle of the stadium I saw Lucia and Gale badly hurt in a corner, but Lucia noticed me luckily she never looked. Some of our guards were in the cells, others dead, but a lot on their knees. I could see Gerard' brother and his wife within the crowd, probably being used as bait to keep Gerard in line.

Morgan spoke first, "Oh Gerard, this is so bittersweet, I mean you were a great leader and lover but your love of those things," she pointed over to Gale and Lucia, so she hated witches, even better. "It's disgusting." She spat then another male came up next to her.

"Morgan," He brought her in for an extremely hot and passionate kiss, I would only imagine that's what I would do if I could ever get that close to Gerard. He then went over and kicked Gerard who flew to the wall. That's when I noticed the slice around his neck, it was deep, so deep he was going to die. He could even be near death now; he was barely healing. This was planned well to weaken him that much.

I was not going to let them get away with this. I moved down in front of Gerard in my wolf form.

"What is that!"

"It's the witch, she shouldn't have this much power left! Guards kill her!"

A lot of guards started coming at us, Lucia had that worried look of hers. Turning to them I bared my teeth and burned some of the guards that were coming to attack us. That made everyone stop, but I couldn't dally, Gerard needed help now. With one easy leap, I jumped onto him and pulled him down where no one could reach us.

"Gerard, wake up." Being back in my own form I slapped him, luckily he didn't look too pissed.

"How are you even here? You were almost drained of all your strength. We all felt it when you left. I was certain they killed you in your sleep."

"I promise I will explain everything later but right now you need to heal." I placed my hands over his neck to start healing him, but he pulled them away.

"Even if you heal me, I need blood," I looked at him. I had never tried this before, but I knew he was right.

I pulled my hair over one shoulder, "I'll try not to kill you."

He smirked, but quickly wrapped one arm around my body pulling me in close and cupped his other large hand around my neck pulling me close to his mouth. I felt his teeth elongate then pierce into my skin. I had to immediately start concentrating to pull my magic out of the blood before entering his system, otherwise, it could kill him, or at least paralyze him. The problem though was vampires released endorphins that put you in a state of euphoria and relaxation. It was hard to not succumb to it. I felt his hands tighten when I started to lose focus snapping me back. He finished quickly and pulled away, but he never let me out of his grasps.

"I'm sorry," he said, then leaned in and kissed me softly on the lips. It didn't last long before he pulled me away. "I need to get out of here, they will kill everyone if I don't kill them first."

"There are too many of them, I have an idea, but I do need some time."

"I'm pretty sure I can handle that." He was smirking again, then he moved his hand to cusp the side of my face. I smiled at him before I pushed him back out, out into the surface. I on the other hand had to go deep, very deep.

CHAPTER NINE

It kept getting darker, I could feel the coldness swarm around me, the chills were crawling up my spine, but I needed to keep going otherwise my little found peace would be stolen from me, again.

I hit the bottom and started walking until I reached the black doors. Behind here lay the leader of all the darkness, the bumps in the night, your nightmares in your dreams, these things could control you and you wouldn't even know it.

I took a deep breath and opened the door, immediately greeted with the smell of mold and decay. I didn't waste time, I rushed in, running past all the shadow creatures until I hit the King's chair. I knelt down on one knee and looked away.

"Father," I looked back up, he was glaring down with eyes so dark it would seem he had nothing in his eye sockets. When he stood, he would be taller no matter how tall you were. His arms and legs were lengthy, his fingers could slice you open with one swift blow. He had no features to look at, he was nothing but darkness, and even if you could get a hit on him, it would pass through him like black smoke.

"Why have you come, *daughter*," He spoke only to the mind, he had no mouth to speak from.

"Father we need your help, the desert people have come and there are too many of them, we need to force them back, or at least leave an impression to stop them from ever coming back." I looked around, motioning that his followers could fill this task.

"You know we don't deal with the top world's dilemmas," he reached out and cupped my face in the same spot that Gerard touched, he had left a Shadow that my father could see. "He stole your heart and blood."

"No father, I gave it to him, well maybe not the heart that kind of just developed, but I promised to protect him and Galen, and all the others." I stared into the emptiness, he has this canny ability to bring up your own darkness with just a look, but I had to work past my nightmares, otherwise, he would never agree.

"If you want help, then just take it," he left to sit back at his throne, leaning in watching what I'll do.

This was a challenge, just like the darkness doesn't ask permission but takes back the shadows in the absence of light. This was a true test of my powers, to see if I can control the creatures under his control. As I turned around, I saw the same figured creatures gather around us, waiting to see what their great lord would do.

I closed my eyes searching for what I needed, diving in deep, where my hate was, I hated that my mother died, I hated Morgan who tried to hurt those close to me, I hated those who hunted me, not just because I was a witch, but for sport. Bringing these feelings forward I felt the aura around me darken, I could start to feel the creatures around me, I felt their bodies as my own and when I opened my eyes I saw what they saw.

It was me standing with a black haze, and eyes as dark as their own, my own eyes were now as dark as my father's, almost like I didn't have eyes at all.

"GO!" They screeched and hollered and obeyed as they started towards the surface. I faced back at my father, he nodded in approval, then I left to deal with what seemed like a big problem to just a tiny nuisance.

I cascaded the fight with wind, rain, and lightning. As we made our way to the surface, I heard the thunder and the lightning strike down. I climbed out of the Shadows first, everyone stopped as I stood there with the rain beating against us.

"Kill her!" Morgan screamed it to her men, but they did not move. I was something they had never seen before, it scared them, and secretly I liked it.

"Rise!" I yelled out and all the shadow creatures rose out of the ground.

People started running and screaming but there was nowhere to go, their blood spilled to the ground before they even knew they were hit. I looked above and forced the lightning down onto those holding Lucia captive. They burst into nothing, leaving only black soot on the ground.

Turning I could see this fight truly was nothing, but a nuisance and the real plan here was of my fathers, I have no doubt he put this idea into their heads. He would want more from me now, the only reason he infatuated my mother was to create a strong offspring.

The fight was over quickly, and their force was dead, all but Morgan and her new lover. They were dragged to me, placed on their knees to answer to their crimes.

"You get one chance." She answered only by spitting at my feet. I was two seconds from turning her to ash before Gerard grabbed my arm. He stopped me and I felt those feelings of love and infatuation take hold. This took me out of my hate, and I started to lose control, the shadow creatures started to scream and retreated back under. They were gone but the rain continued.

"Guards, grab them" he ordered this without ever taking his eyes off me.

Men came and took them away; they didn't fight but obediently took their chains and left. They would be tortured for information and for the sins they committed.

"I'm not even sure where to begin with you. The power your

blood gave me, or the monsters you have risen from the ground."

"Well, I assure you the power boost is new to me. I didn't know that would happen. The monsters were a surprise too."

"Only the Lord of the Shadow Realm can control them, or should I dare say, *an heir*." I smiled at him, I didn't need to tell him. "Full of surprises, one thing I don't believe I will ever understand is why you really let me take you that day in the woods."

"I'm strong, but I'm not fast. The moment it takes me to sum up the power I need to cast is the moment it takes you to kill me. I keep telling you this, but you keep not believing me, besides you've kind of grown on me." I grabbed the front of his shirt to pull him in for a kiss. He wrapped his arms around me to pull me in and passionately kissed me back.

I knew from this moment on I would forever protect this little piece of happiness I had found, for as long as I can.

Well, it's been a passing of a full moon; I know Gerard is safe over in the Desert lands with his guards because they constantly send messages back stating so. I was very insistent that I go too but he profusely denied my persistence and made me stay behind to protect his home. We haven't actually been able to sit and talk about what happened between us since everything. The Dessert King had no idea what his little brother was up to and demanded his return so he could punish him. Gerard and he had come to an arrangement and now he is there and I am stuck here.

"No matter how long you stare out that window he will not show up in his bedroom," I turned to look at Lucia

"How would you know, he is super fast," we both laughed to break the tension.

I didn't like how long he has been gone, his sister has been in charge and luckily, she has changed her tune since I saved their lives, but still, this place without him just feels empty.

"I think we need to do something fun. We have done nothing

but train and worry all this time. You have barely left the house." Lucia was staring me down.

"They look at me like I'm a monster. Not a witch, nor human, nor vampire. How else am I supposed to respond?"

"Like you know it and you're fine with it. You have a lot more power in your one pinky than I do in my whole body. Besides, if you still will not take my word for it, think how Gerard reacted to you when he saw you all evil-like." She was grinning, she got me there. Gerard looked when he grabbed my arm and never looked away, that caught me. He was looking at me like I became so important to him that he would even go to the Shadow King himself to have me.

"Fine, one outing for half the day, that is all you get."

She threw her hands over me and dragged me into a hug and all at the same time pulled me out of my seat. She became very comfortable with bossing me around, not that I minded she gave me something I had never had before, a friend.

We decided to head into the manor, see if we could borrow one of the carriages we could possibly go to town with. Going into the hall where they hold their galas, we found Galen.

"Hey, Galen!" I yelled, he immediately turned and ran to us.

"Hey! You finally came out of hiding," Lucia laughed but I just rolled my eyes.

"Ok guys thanks for reminding me that I became a hermit."

"So, Galen now that I got her out, we were hoping to use a carriage?"

"Why would you leave now? My uncle is coming home soon." I froze, I wanted him home but the thought of him finally here again, well that just made me extremely nervous.

"What do you think Angelic?" She turned to me and I'm sure she could tell how nervous this news made me. "Hey Galen, yeah we want to head into town. She could probably use the extra time to compose herself."

Galen laughed, "Yes I suppose she does."

"Alright we get it, I'm nervous, I can't help it."

"Well, I suppose you guys could use one, but I would be back before nightfall. Gerard will probably be here before then and if you're gone for too long he might not be happy."

"I don't think I mind making him wait a few extra hours considering I have had to wait for a whole passing of the full moon."

"Alright, I'll tell one of the guards to bring it out front."

"Thanks, Galen, I will see you later."

"Ok, be safe!"

We left for the front gates while he went to ask one of the guards. People were busy getting everything ready for tonight. I suppose Isabella is making sure everything was set when her brother returned.

"Lucia, what am I going to do? I feel like I'm completely stumbling over myself while he is so composed."

"Well, I suppose he's probably also quite lost. He lost his so-claimed mate to betrayal and now he's become infatuated with a Witch. Vampires use witches for their powers, not for their feelings."

"Yeah, you're right. Well, I suppose if I screw up too badly, I can just disappear."

"I would never forgive you. If you leave me here alone, I will personally follow you and drag you back." I threw one of my arms around her shoulders and laughed. She truly was one of the best things to happen to me.

We arrived at the front gates and the carriage was already there waiting for us. Apparently, Galen works fast because I didn't think it took us that long to get here.

"I'm going to get you to pull the carriage, keep practicing on your focus," Lucia simply rolled her eyes at me and hopped onto the driver seat and I followed behind her. We were then off down the road to town.

"Do you think we should grab a drink while we're down there?" Lucia asked

"I don't see why not, not that there is much else to do

anyway." I smiled back at her. It was nice to just be free like this knowing no one is going to hunt us or try to catch us. We can try to just be normal witches for a change and enjoy the winter air.

Coming into town was full of hustle and bustle. There were a lot of people running around, probably gossiping about the Gala events. Knowing that their King is gone is probably making everyone a bit more on edge.

"Halt!" It was Rig I recognized his voice immediately.

Lucia slowed the carriage down to a stop and Rig and Kai came up to us.

"What are you two doing down here?"

"We were permitted the day off and we decided to enjoy it by grabbing a drink at the tavern." We both held firm, any spot of weakness and they would think we were lying.

"Fine, go ahead." They backed off from us and we continued down the road.

It wasn't too far when we made it up the small hill and hit the ole tavern. It really wasn't much but it had a bit of charm on it. Possibly done by a witch many generations ago. We both hopped down and went into the musty building. There were only a few others here, mostly vampires, probably because humans were working and, well you just never saw witches out much. We found a seat by the bar and ordered our drinks.

"What do you want to drink too?" I asked.

"How about to the celebration that I finally got you out of the house." We taped our glasses together and took a swig.

"We probably shouldn't stay out too late otherwise it will probably make the guard suspicious."

"I don't think I would particularly care if I made those two suspicious." Lucia shook her head at my answer. "Why don't we get some food! Bartender! Can we get two of your specials please?"

"Of course!" He yelled, then disappeared into the back.

We stayed for a few hours, getting louder and louder the more we drank and ate. It was fun to be out with a friend, but it was almost nightfall. We decided to tip our bartender and head out.

It had started to snow on our way home, once we were out of the town, I produced a small flame to help keep us warm.

"Now that is something I could use, both for me and Galen."

"And you probably can, you're advancing well and I'd say you would probably get it in about a year."

"A year!"

I laughed at her, "Yes a year. Flame is extremely tricky and the moment you lose focus on it, it will spread and become out of control."

"Oh, fine then but I will learn it."

"And I am sure you will, I was going to start teaching you earlier but then all that shit went down, and now here we are." I smiled at her.

We were getting through the thicker portion of the forest when we heard noises coming from behind us. Did it sound like a runaway cart?

We both looked behind and saw a carriage going at full speed towards us. I pulled our carriage out of the way just in time to see this one pass us and continue towards the castle. We didn't waste any time. I took control, and we were going to catch up no matter what.

We were just outside the Manor when it slowed down and more gracefully pulled up to the entrance. We slowly crept up behind it and jumped down and waited to see who would get out.

The door opened and a larger old man came out. He was a mage for sure, powerful, definitely stronger than Gale. Then a young woman came out, lean, blonde, beautiful, she was a higher-class vampire. Then one more man came through and I recognized him from the Gala. He was one of the ministers from out of town, a vampire as well.

The mage came towards us, "Bow down to your superiors."

Lucia and I just looked at each other and tried not to laugh, "Sorry, but there is only one Master we bow to and it's not you."

He actually got mad and he started to charge his power, I could feel the electricity in the air. He plunged at Lucia, but I immediately got in the way and put forth a barrier, his spell only sizzled and died.

"That is enough!" We all looked over and my stomach dropped, and I froze, it was Gerard.

He looked exhausted, and he was definitely hungry, but he walked down the front steps with authority challenging us to continue, but this mage only backed off and went back to the older vampire.

"Welcome Carlton," He shook his hand, "And this must be your daughter Ivy." He then took her hand and kissed it. This guy certainly knows how to strike a nerve.

I decided I was not going to continue to watch and turned around and started walking home.

"Angelic stop!" I was mad, my power was spilling out and if I didn't calm down it would come out with a force that would hurt everyone around here, but because he is supposed to be my owner I stopped and turned my head. "I expect to see you later." I nodded my head then continued towards my home as they went into the manor.

Lucia joined them, I heard Gerard tell her Galen was looking for her. This worked out for me because I needed to be alone. Getting back home I made some chamomile tea to calm me down. I wanted to escape, and I should not have been surprised that he would have had another suitor waiting. He is a Vampire King and I am nothing but a witch in his eyes.

I sat at the table and decided to read a book. It had started to snow, and I started a fire in our fireplace. It was nice to be in my own little world for a while; but then there was a knock on the door, and it was a bit of a surprise to me that he came here.

"Come in," he waited in politeness, that was all.

"I see you finally calmed down," He sat in the chair opposite of me.

"Sorry about that I didn't mean to cause a scene."

"Yes you did n't lie to me, but I believe I could understand why. There are some situations I have to deal with, and I don't need my own witch to start misbehaving."

"So that's it then, your witch, protect the king, after what happened I expected a bit more from you."

"You should know very well why what happened can't happen again. We are worlds apart. I live in a different world than you."

I got up from my seat, I didn't believe him, he was burying his feelings. I walked over to him and leaned against the table right in front of him. Using air, I created a small cut on my neck.

"You're exhausted and hungry, drink, then you can continue on with your lies."

He looked at me so intensely, but he stood up towering over me. Reaching around he grabbed my hair and pulled it back exposing my neck, I felt his other arm pull around my back and pulled me in closer, my body molded into his, his lips came down to my neck. He didn't hesitate and bit in quite fiercely. I knew he was hungry but not this hungry. Drinking greedily, he made this harder than it should be. We both started to lose focus and he had to pull back from the new onset of pain. Stepping away he wiped his mouth; I took a cloth and wiped my neck and healed the wound.

He was facing away from me now, looking at his hands, "Gerard I..."

When he turned around his eyes were the brightest red I had ever seen, "The power that you give me is astounding. I had not had a drink since the last. I never even realized how hungry I was until you bled."

"I'm sorry Gerard," he came over and cupped the side of my face before coming close and kissing me. I tried kissing back, but he pulled away too fast.

"For now, I will have to deal with the suitors coming in. A witch and a vampire are unheard of."

"To be fair I'm not a witch."

"And we will keep that a secret." I nodded to him, that would be a dangerous secret to spread.

"I will be here if you need me," I bowed down in respect.

"I know," he then disappeared back outside into the snow.

So, in the coming days, we will be getting more and more suiters coming in to steal Gerard' heart, but I have no intention of letting any one of them anywhere near his heart or soul.

CHAPTER TEN

The next few days were just complete hell. There were at least five suitors here with their sleazy parents and their witches. Which all believed they were better than the rest. I don't think I get vampires, why are they in charge, they care nothing but power and greed.

Gerard was hiding in his study when I finally found him. He was just sitting there towering over his papers. He didn't even notice me, or maybe he did.

I knocked on the door first, "Hey, you wanted to see me?"

"Yes, come in and shut the door."

I did as I was told and took the seat in front of his desk. He wasn't looking at me yet but was finishing writing whatever he was doing first.

"We have an influx of mages here and there starting to become arrogant. They all believe they are stronger than the other." I just nodded, "I need them handled." He was just staring at me.

"Wait, you want me to figure out what to do with them?"

"Yes, that is your area. I am expected to keep things in order, but I am too busy with other plans to deal with them, so the responsibility falls on you."

"You owe me for this," He just smiled at me and waved me off. "Fine, get them all to meet me outside in the courtyard after supper."

"Very well, and Angelic, no Shadow work."

"You just like to take the fun out of it all don't you?"

He stood up and came behind me, leaning down he wrapped his arms around me, coming in close to my neck he started to softly place his lips on my skin, causing me to shiver in response. His touch was very electrifying. His hands started to come around lingering down by my waist. The moment his fingers touched my stomach, I felt a knot, and this was just a bit too much for me right now.

"Ok! I will get that started for you." I stood up out of my chair and he laughed going back to his chair.

I was still breathing a little harder than I should have been, of course, I wanted him, but I have never had these feelings before. He does something to my body when he touches it.

Heading outside I saw three of the suitors talking to one of the guards. They must be wanting to go to town.

"You!" I recognized her from before, it was Ivy.

I walked up to them only out of politeness, "Hello."

"I need you to get us a carriage and take us to town. We need to grab some items before our formal introductions with Lord Gerard."

"As much as I would love to help, I can not. I have a task to complete for Master Gerard." I knew they couldn't argue with me on this, but I felt like they really wanted to try.

"Witch, if you refuse now, I swear to you when he picks me, you will no longer be needed. Kyle is much stronger than you. Can you even pull a carriage?"

"Have a great day ladies," I could only walk away from the stupid in these women. They have no idea what I am capable of. Every guard, vampire, and human that was there that day was sworn to silence.

I ended up finding Lucia puttering away in the garden. She

has grown to be quite strong and I think it's time she actually faces a challenge.

"Lucia, I have a proposition for you."

"Galen warned me you might ask something of me, and he said no."

"Oh come on! Is everyone against me today?"

She laughed, "No Ava but you're going to have to deal with them on your own."

"I just thought it would be a good opportunity to see how well you advanced. There are five of them, and five against one isn't very fair." She just rolled her eyes at me and continued to garden.

"I think he just wants to see what you can do besides Shadow work."

"How did you know I can't use Shadow spells?"

"Galen told me, should have warned me."

"Ok fine, but if I get hurt, I'm blaming all of you."

"I doubt you will, but what will you do?"

"Only way to settle an ego is to talk some sense into them, and if that doesn't work, beat it out of them."

"I think I will go make some tea and you should come up with a plan."

"Sure Lucia, I'll come inside in just a minute."

I turned my attention to the Manor. It didn't take me long to find Gerard. He was in the dining hall with a bunch of people. I believe it was the mix of the mages and ministers. The suitors seemed to have found a way to town. There was something bothering me though. If I did this there was a chance I could be caught but I had to look into it.

I went down to my cat because it had a lot more stealth than a wolf. I found my way into the dining hall, and I was right that all of them were in here. Gerard was discussing with the other mages that they would be required to meet me outside later. After they would all get together and he would meet each suiter.

"Lord Gerard, are you still going to go with the old traditions?"

"What do you mean Minister Carlton?"

"Well my mage is extremely powerful; I doubt there is one in here that could beat him. If my mage beats yours will you take my daughter's hand?"

"Carlton, if any one of the mages beats Angelic, I will take their daughter's hand." He smiled then looked down at me. This was crazy. He just challenged me to beat all of them. I flicked my tail at him and left.

I went back home and sat with Lucia, the tea she makes always helps me calm my nerves.

"What happened?"

"It's Gerard! He just challenged all the minister's mages to beat me in a battle. If one wins, he will Marry their daughter immediately." I plopped my head on the table.

"He must have a lot of faith in you to determine his fate."

I had never thought of that, this would put him in a big predicament if I failed. I took a big drink of my tea.

"Alright then, Lucia I'm going into my room to focus for a while, just let me know when everyone is out in the courtyard," she nodded.

I retreated into my bedroom and I would not come out until it was time to deal with these insects. They will not win, not when Gerard put his future in my hands.

It was almost nightfall when I felt Lucia call for me. She and the others were all waiting in the courtyard. I could sense an urgency in her call. They must think I won't show up. Getting up from my bed I made my way out, they would be in for a very big surprise.

Coming into their view everyone pulled away from their conversation and turned towards me. I wasn't what you would call threatening, but I started to pulse out power, trying to push fear into their minds. They would know I am dangerous. The power radiating off me is not even comprehensible to their own.

"Welcome," I put a big smile on my face.

The other mages came forward. Their masters and the suitors stayed back. Galen and Lucia were here watching too, and of course, Gerard was standing with his arms crossed. He wanted to see what I would do without Shadow work.

"You don't scare us witches, we know your tricks."

They started to pulse out their own power. It felt like a tickle on my skin, barely even comparable.

"Prepare yourself, witch."

He was collecting electricity, along with the others. They were all going to attack at the same time. When they all set out their attack, I could see in slow motion the lightning coming towards me. This will hurt but I want them to know that I can take a hit.

I put my arms in front of me and let them take the brunt of the hit. This force pushed me back a few feet and the burns were extraordinarily painful, but I would heal and then it would be my turn.

Watching their faces become confused as I still stood was very satisfying. I showed them that not only can I survive a strong attack but all of their forces together did not take me down.

"Are you sure you want to continue?"

"You don't scare us."

"Very well."

I decided to use the snow to my advantage, causing the wind to create a snowstorm from the ground up. The snow blew around us causing everyone to cover their eyes. I never moved, the snow never got close enough, but I could see where everyone was and what they were up to.

A couple had started to create barriers around themselves, which was good, it steals some of their focus. The other three were trying to use their own wind and keep the snow away from them.

I saw a shot of fire heading towards me, it was coming from

Kyle, he had something to prove and would make this a lot more annoying than it needed to be. I forced the fireball away and it moved past me without even making me flinch. There were other fire shots coming at me from different angles. I don't see how if they defeat me how they will choose who actually did it.

I moved the fire shots away just as easily as the first. "This is pointless, just surrender and we can all go inside for a warm cup of tea."

It was only then that I noticed the tree limbs come up from the ground and wrap around my legs, dragging me upside down in front of them.

"What were you saying about surrendering?"

I let the winter storm die and now it was easy to see the clear night sky and the moon was almost full casting a beautiful glow.

"This is annoying." I looked over at Gerard who shook his head. Still, no Shadow work allowed, and I can't go inside his head, so what did he leave me with.

I was about to make my next move when everything went darker, the shadows stretched out, and the sky seemed to dim even with the full moon. Everyone lost focus and I was released from the roots hold and fell to the ground. I didn't move. I knew they were coming, just like before.

"Angelic, what are you doing?" Gerard yelled out

"It's not me, trust me."

"Mages go to your masters."

Everyone started to move back to their owners getting in front of them waiting for these things to reveal themselves. Lucia held onto Galen' hand and Gale was in front of them both. I did not move closer to Gerard though, but he decided to come to me.

"Gerard, you should stay back, they're here for me."

"I will not give up my own witch. If they are here for you then they will have to deal with me."

"And here I thought I was supposed to protect you."

He turned to me and smiled, "Now, whatever gave you that impression."

They started to crawl out of the shadows of the trees and crawling out of the darkened ground. They were nothing but black silhouettes, towering over most, giving off a menacing smile.

"It is time you come with usssss, young one." He spoke slowly, taking care to sound out every syllable.

"She will not be going anywhere." Gerard stood in front of me and the creatures backed up, only a little.

Everyone was frozen-still; they knew these creatures existed but never would have seen one. They can make the bravest man crumble down into a scared child.

"She belongs with us, Vampire."

One came up from the ground beside me, grabbing my arm. Their touch always burned the skin leaving dark marks. These creatures wouldn't be affected by magic or brute force, or at least none that I have figured out yet. He pulled me away towards the darkened forest.

"Ava!" I heard Lucia scream.

Gerard started coming towards us, "Let her go creature!" but it never stopped and continued to the forest. I tried to pull away, but the grip would only get tighter every time I tried. "I said, LET HER GO!"

Immediately the creature let me go, when it turned to look at its hand, he looked confused, he didn't even realize he had done it. That just made a lot of new questions arise.

"Leave here!" Gerard yelled and the creatures looked confused, almost as if they weren't sure what they were supposed to do.

"We will return to the King, see you again *our* dear Angelic." He dragged out my name with the last of it lingering in the air as they disappeared. The land glowed with the light of the moon again. Everyone was frozen and waited for Gerard to speak. My arm still had the black mark of his grip.

"Everyone back to your rooms."

"My Lord I think we should return back to the dining hall, let us discuss tonight's events," Carlton said

"Minister, I don't know if this threat is over or not, I would feel more comfortable if you and your family returned to your rooms." Gerard turned to Gale, "Gale I need you to get the guards out and around the perimeter, make sure they are all gone. Lucia, take Galen back to his room and stay with him." They both bowed to him and everyone started heading out in different directions.

He wasn't facing me but from behind, I could see he was tense, he was confused also, he knew they listened to him. He never turned to me when he spoke.

"Angelic, go to my room; I will meet you there shortly."

"Gerard, I don't think that would be a good idea."

"Do as I say Angelic. I don't need you disobeying me right now."

"Of course." I headed inside and when I turned around, he was already gone.

Inside was busy, everyone was running around, many humans heading back to the common areas, guards heading outside. No one paid much attention to me as I slipped past them and headed into Gerard's bedroom. Not much had changed from the last time I was here. Looking out his window still had a perfectly good view of my snow-covered home.

He had some papers spread out on his desk, most of it was about the suitors. What their strengths and weaknesses are; what possible issues they could have. There was one mark on here that seemed odd though, it had a positive or negative next to it. Ivy's name had a positive on it, now what could that mean? This also means he is a list-orientated vampire, interesting.

"Having fun going through my things?" I turned to see him standing at his door. He never moved closer or took his eyes off me.

"I wasn't speaking, it was just lying there." He moved to sit on the edge of his bed. I did not dare move; he was on edge from these events.

"Come here," I walked over to him slowly and when I got close enough, he grabbed my arm, and lightly fell over the black marks. "Why aren't these healing?"

"It always takes longer to heal from their touch." Feeling his touch made me inexplicably aware of how he made me feel. I felt the longing to get closer to him.

"You know I can't stay; he will just keep coming back putting more people in danger."

He moved so fast I barely noticed what happened, he pulled me down onto his bed, lying flat on my back. He was over top of me, holding down my arms above my head.

"I am pretty sure I'm the one that says when you can leave." He started to give small kisses along my neck. I moved my head to the side instinctively, barely realizing that I had.

I tried to move my legs up, but he used his weight to keep me flat, he continued down to my collar, and I felt his fangs pierce my skin before I could even protest. He let go of my arms but wrapped one around me pulling me up closer, molding me into his body. My concentration was waning, and I could tell he could feel it, but he didn't stop. My lips parted. I needed him to stop before I would lose myself completely.

"Tell me, what are the positives next to your suitors names?" He clenched harder before releasing me, he got up off the bed wiping his mouth. I didn't really want him to stop but this question keeps burning in my mind.

"I'm not sure that is something you would really like to know."

I sat on the side of the bed holding onto his lingering bite mark, not saying a word.

"Very well then, if you really want to know, it is who has the capabilities of producing an heir."

"I see." He's right, I didn't really want to know that. Only reminding me of why he needs to be with one of them and not me. "I wasn't lying when I said I needed to go. I just need to talk to him, I am not staying down there."

He was looking down at his list, "And how long is it you think you need?"

"If I have my way, a day, but I fear it is more like a week."

Gerard sighed, "Very well," He came back over to me and cupped my face, leaning in kissing me. This time I got to kiss him back, but I had to pull away this time.

"I will come back, just try to keep from picking a suitor, otherwise I won't come back." He started laughing, it was a nice thing to hear before leaving him. "Goodbye, Gerard." He stepped back and this time I just turned to smoke in front of him, and when I reappear it will be in front of the Shadow Kings castle.

CHAPTER ELEVEN

Staring up at *his* castle gave me nothing but old memories of dark nightmares. After coming out from the shadow realm when I was a child, I realized my mother was gone. There were a lot of vampires around lurking, looking for me. They knew she had a child, but they didn't know that child was also the daughter of the Shadow king. He has no loyalty, only to himself. I believe he doesn't even see me as anything but a tool.

I was on the other side of the bridge staring at his black castle. If you look down, you will see nothing but a bottomless pit. I had always thought Gerard' mansion was overdone but now staring at my fathers' home, Gerard's home was nothing but as small as mine and Lucia's home. His creatures were lurking around in the corners. Staring back into the forest, they were peaking around the trees. I wouldn't be able to linger too long or they'd just drag me in any way. I took one step onto the bridge and the doors cracked open, no one could physically open these large doors, you had to be welcomed or expected.

I had been here enough to know my way to the throne room, it had never changed. Stepping in he was sitting there peering down. He had no face to show an expression. I kneeled on one knee, as expected of everyone who entered.

"You summoned me, father."

He got up from his throne and as he descended, he turned to his humanoid figure. He wore black robes with gray seams, where it crossed in the front it exposed a lot of his chest, you could see his long black hair flowing around his back, and his face had the features of a young man, but his eyes only reflected his old black soul.

"My daughter." I stood when he got close, and he wrapped his arms around me; I did not return the gesture. "What is this?" Gerard' bite.

"It is nothing father. What have you summoned me for?"

"You have been gone too long, and now you're letting these things slither deeper into your mind and body. You are as much a part of me as you were your mother, and I do not condone your fascination with this vampire."

"My fascination," I pulled away from him, "With that vampire has nothing to do with you; and how would you know what she would have agreed or disagreed with."

"I knew her far longer than your short years with her." That hurt, to think he got to be with my mother longer, knowing what kind of monster he is, it broke my heart. The worst part is wondering why my mother let him. "I think it is time you stayed here, time to take some responsibilities for what you truly are."

"I'm not like you."

He smiled at me, causing a very unnerving feeling, "No? Then what about Liam? Surely you don't think I would not have noticed."

"I said I'm not like you, not that I am not incapable of using the abilities you gave me from being your cursed daughter."

He was very amused by my outbursts, "Why don't you just stay in your room for a while until you calm down." He started to walk away from me, calling for his creatures to come take me.

"I'm not staying!"

I collected every bit of energy I could and shot it at him. His humanoid state could be injured, and I wanted to hurt him. I wanted to make sure he knew I was being very serious.

He turned quickly and caught the ball of energy, "Very cute." It started to sizzle down into nothing.

I ran for him if magic won't work then what about his own power against him. I jumped at him, latching onto his arms. All I needed was contact and we would dive down deep into his own mind.

"You have no power here." He was still very calm and poised.

"And how can you be sure we are in my mind and not in your own?" He started to create an evil grin. Then there was screaming, it was my mother's.

I saw someone that looked like Gerard drinking from my mother, he was going to continue until he killed her. Lucia was being brutally murdered by Galen. He wouldn't let me look away from this scene, and when I closed my eyes it would just reappear there. He had me trapped, and I wouldn't be able to leave until he let me.

My mother lay dead on the floor and Gerard dripping with her blood, my father moved towards him and he did not stir. "You are in love with this?" He continued to look down at Gerard like he was a pathetic flea. The next thing I saw was my father ripping Gerard' heart out, and he joined my mother on the ground. "That would have been so much more satisfying if it was the real thing."

Everything looked so real, there screams, the pleadings, he created these images to torture my heart. I felt tears form but I could not let them fall, he would see it as a weakness and beat me for it.

He stood in front of me, grabbing my jaw, forcing me to look up at him, "Do not ever think you can overpower me, behave, and I will not make this as torturous for you as I do for others."

When he let go, we were back in his throne room. His creatures grabbed my arms and started forcing me out back to the room I thought I had escaped from him so many years ago.

The castle hadn't changed much, still the same cold stone, with photos of destruction and fire. Some would have a beautiful image, but it would be eerie if you looked at it for too long. We were coming up to a picture of a beautiful woman, but her eyes would always be staring at you no matter which angle you were looking at it.

I hurried along until we hit the red door, my room. I had insisted on a coloured door, and he told me if I could survive three days of a tortured mind without going crazy he would let me. Thinking of the images that were presented to me back then made me shiver.

They opened the door and forced me in, shutting it behind them. I knew it would be locked, and even if I unlocked it, he would return me back into his psychotic nightmare.

The room really hadn't changed much, the window still looked out over the forest, a bed, dresser, desk, and a bathroom. He put that in here because he didn't want to give me an excuse to leave my room.

I needed to get out of here, I would go mad if I continued to look at these walls. My hope is that Lucia was asleep. Resting on my bed, refusing to get under the covers, I fell asleep, hoping to do something I have not done in a long time.

Fortunately, it didn't take me long to sleep and Lucia was indeed asleep. I saw her standing on a grassy hill under a beautiful clear day and the sun shining bright. It was refreshing to see it, compared to the darkness here or the last month of colder weather.

She saw me starting to walk towards her, "Ava! Please tell me it's really you."

"It's me." When I reached her, we embraced each other in a big hug.

"What happened, Gerard said you had to leave."

"I had to go see my father. He would have continued, and

next time I doubt he would have been so nice." We sat on the grass, it was a nice break and made me excited for the spring. "Tell me what is going on back home?"

"That Ivy girl is clinging, she told him to send the others home because can give him everything he needs. I think he keeps the others around just to keep her distracted, but also now that you're gone her father is letting him use Kyle whenever he needs."

"That's a laugh, she really is pushing it isn't she." I pulled some grass mindlessly tearing at it.

"I think he worries; I mean it's been three days with no news from you."

"What! Already! Damn, I hate this place." I fell to the ground laying there staring up at the sky. I knew time moved differently here, but I didn't think it was that bad. Did he purposely leave us in my mind for longer than I thought? I closed my eyes and thought of Gerard, the way he smiled, laughed, scowled at me when I said the wrong things.

"Just leave, what is even holding you there?"

I turned on my side to look at her, propping my head up with my arm, "I can't yet, I know he wants something, he just won't tell me right away."

"Then you need to hurry, it's not just the suitors who are trying to weave their ways in with the King. The fathers are pushing their favors in too, Galen tells me of all their bribery."

"Trust me, Lucia, I will move as fast as I can. I'll leave you to rest now." She hugged me one more time before I blinked and opened my eyes in my darkroom.

Showering and dressing in a beautiful black gown, I walked down for dinner. Corridors filled with nothing but black space. The creatures would lurk in different corners giving some movements in the shadows, but they were all the same, empty.

The dining hall is exactly what you would expect, a big empty room with a giant ass table in the middle. Though there was a fire going, and it was quite a beautiful fireplace with all the stonework around it. I sat at my end of the table and waited for my father. Even though he doesn't eat, if I started without him, he would probably cut my tongue out.

I heard the doors open and he walked in, in his humanoid figure. At least he is trying to be slightly more comfortable, not by much. He took his seat at the end of his table where the same plate of food that I have was placed in front of him.

I watched the steam rise from the concoction of meat and vegetables swimming in its broth. I hated stew, yet he thought it was my favorite. He never knew what I liked, or he did and just did the opposite for sport.

"Going to play the starvation game again?" I glared back at him and reluctantly grabbed my spoon and took a bite. He only just smiled and actually started to eat his as well.

As soon as I was done, I stood and walked out of the room. I absentmindedly walked to the front gates. They won't open for me. He would never let me leave since the last time I got lost in those woods. I was young and naïve.

It was shortly after my mother was murdered that my father came to collect me. He brought me down to his throne room and he told me who he was, at the time I was grateful that I even had a father. He let me off easy for a while, but he didn't like my carefree self or how my mother raised me. It was cold that day, possibly mid-winter on the surface. He told me I needed to learn the truth and be prepared for the evils that were in us. He showed me his true form and I was horrified, so I ran into the woods hoping to hide from him, instead, all I found were nightmares. There are many different kinds of creatures here, and they would have torn me apart if he didn't come after me. I remember hiding behind trees, pulling into the shadows. He scared them off or ordered them too. When he came to me, he really looked worried, he went back to his human form and carried me back home. I remember peeking over his shoulder sticking my tongue out at everything that watched us, I thought he was my hero after that until he wasn't.

I just shook my head at the memory, it was long ago, and things were different now. I needed to figure out what he wanted so I could get back home.

Everything was on repeat down here. Sleep, eat, argue, repeat. It may have been a month that has gone by on the surface, it was so hard to tell. This dinner was not going any better than the previous ones.

"Just tell me what you want me to do, you usually have some sort of task for me when you go on these slow-moving tortuous games."

"I have no task for you, I am just enjoying the company of my daughter." He was smiling and glaring at me while he took another bite of his meat pie, but then his smile turned into a large grin. "It appears we have a guest."

Generally guest means client. Someone who has found their way here to ask him for a favor and in return servitude. Though this feeling and power was not of a normal visitor, this one had power, and he was getting closer to the dining room. A place my father would never allow visitors in.

"Welcome, Gerard." My father spoke, and as I turned my head to the entrance there he was standing, with one of the shadow creatures behind him. Almost as if he was being ordered by him.

"Angelic you told me a week; it has now been over three."

"I..." I looked back at my father who looked just as insane as ever, grinning.

My father spoke back before I could, "Why don't you join us, there is a lot of food to go around, unless you would rather just quench your thirst." He took another bite of his food, all while another creature pushed a chair out for him.

Surprisingly, he took the seat, and a plate was placed in front of him. "I am not here to play your games; I am only here to take Angelic back to where she belongs."

"But we have had barely any time to catch up."

I glared at him, "We have had plenty of time, you just refuse to tell me what it is you want."

"If you truly don't want to stay with me, then leave, if" He lowered his gaze. "He can get one of them to return you both to the surface."

There it was, it wasn't my test, it was for Gerard. He wanted to see how much he could control them. Gerard stood then.

"We will be leaving then." He looked back at the same creature he walked in with, "You, we are leaving, take us back to the surface."

It had immediately started walking over to him. I stood up as fast as I could and ran to him. I was not going to stay behind.

"Very well then," He tipped his glass at us, "Until next time." He started grinning again while drinking. We turned and left before anything else could be said or done.

We were directed out to the front gate, and on the other side was a free-standing door. He opened it for us, it was just a black gate, but once the creature placed its hand on the opening the scene changed to Gerard' manor. Gerard walked first, and the thing even bowed to him. Going in after him it felt like a light breeze as I made it into the other side.

The snow had melted and there was a blue sky with light clouds. It was a gorgeous day. I could not wait to see Lucia.

"I suppose a thank you is in order."

Gerard turned to me. "Oh, you will trust me, but right now you need to go home. She has done nothing but nag me, even got Galen in on it." I could not help but laugh, I bowed a bit before bolting to my house.

The grass was completely drenched from the melted snow. It splashed up my backside, soaking my whole back before I reached the house. I almost made it to the door knob when the door burst open and I got bear-hugged by a very emotional Lucia. I almost tripped over my own feet as I got dragged inside.

"I can not believe you are back! He told me so many times,

just wait, just wait. I guess his patience must have worn off too." Lucia was practically yelling.

"Could you make some tea? I could really use a batch of your most relaxing, and calming brews."

"Coming right up!" She started getting busy with getting her herbs and dishes together.

Looking around it hadn't changed at all, except there were more herbs in the window and more plants. She has a unique talent for brewing up exactly what people need.

She poured our drinks and sat at the table with me. I wrapped my hands around the warm cup, sniffing up all the smells, it was absolutely wonderful. Cinnamon was definitely one of my favorites.

"I suppose I need to catch you up on some things." I looked at her in bewilderment, until everything came back all at once.

I placed my cup down, depending on what she says I may choke on it, "Go on."

"First things, Gerard did not choose a suitor. In fact, he sort of couldn't. Only Ivy is here now, holding on to hope. She has tried everything! She just can't get a clue" Lucia shrugged her shoulders before taking a sip of her own tea.

"What do you think has held him up?"

"Well, he says it's because he's not ready. That it was too soon to try right after Morgan's betrayal; but we all know why really." She winked at me.

I couldn't help but look down, I could feel the rising heat in my cheeks, though I hoped that was because of the hot tea.

"Now you tell me what happened? Why were you gone for so long? What did he want you to do?

"Honestly nothing, we argued and bickered like normal. I tried so many times to get in his head, which is impossible; but honestly, I don't think he wanted something from me. I believe he was just waiting for Gerard."

"What do you mean?"

"Remember during the fight with the mages, one of the

shadow creatures grabbed my arm, and Gerard yelled at it to stop, and it did?" She nodded her head, "Well I am pretty certain that is what he was waiting for. To see if he would command one of them to come to get me. Though I don't think he thought he could actually go to his realm."

We both were quiet for a bit before Lucia spoke first. "Well, if it is what he wanted, then I suppose you should be on your guard. Who knows what he will try next; but also right now you should probably get cleaned up, they're going to want you at dinner tonight I'm sure."

I groaned, "No more dinners. I just want to stay here and hide for a while."

"You can hide tomorrow. Galen would love to see you."

She got me there, "Okay, fine, I'll go." She was grinning.

"But I will give you your space. I'm going to go tell Galen."

She gave me another bear hug before departing. Looking out of our window I could see Gerard' room. It was dark, which meant he was probably in his study.

The fire cracked loudly making me jump, and my heart pounding. I wasn't even down there that long, in his time, and he already brought back my paranoia. What was worse, I was sure Ivy would be there at dinner tonight, and I am sure she will be all over him.

Making myself presentable wasn't as hard as I thought it would be, a nice pair of boots with black pants, and an off-the-shoulder shirt showed off my figure well. The collar around my neck still hung there. I'm actually quite amazed my father didn't even mention it. I absentmindedly felt around Gerard' symbol crafted in it. Just one more dinner before I can relax for a little while. I grabbed my shawl before heading out.

The manor was quiet, not many around right now. Just as I was coming up to the dining hall, I saw Ivy talking to Gerard, clinging to his arm. They entered together, then behind him was Marcus. He gave me a warm smile.

"Didn't think you would actually make it."

"I would not have if someone wasn't a little pushy." I looked over at Lucia already sitting next to Galen and Cade.

The rest of the crowd was here as well, with Ivy plopping herself right next to Gerard, this will be a very long dinner.

I felt a hand on my back, "Let's go join them, shall we?" Marcus was smiling down at me, he also knew I was tense about the whole situation. I decided to let him lead me to my seat, then he sat right next to me.

The food started coming out immediately and I just looked down at my hands, whether it was out of habit or avoidance I didn't care, this is the last place I wanted to be. A bowl of tomato soup was set down, and I could not be happier.

I felt a kick from across the table and looked up to see Lucia staring at me, "You alright Ava?"

"Yes, I'm fine." I looked over at Gerard who was also staring at me. I just grabbed my spoon and began eating, continuing to avoid everyone's gaze.

Everyone continued talking to each other, talking about their days. Lucia has been working more with herbs, Galen was doing well in his classes, Ivy was pressuring Gerard.

"My god, are you broken?" Ivy spoke very vindictively.

I noticed that it was directed at me. "I'm not broken?" It was a very odd question.

"Well, you just sit there, you should be listening to your Master. Just like a servant witch should be."

I felt my hands go hot and I had to clench them in order to stop the burst of anger. Down in his realm, I didn't need to worry about my outbursts but here I did.

Gerard spoke up first though, "I don't believe it is your concern with what my witch does, if it does not bother me, it certainly should have no effect on you."

"But Gerard if I am your best match as a suitor, I think I would like to know a bit more about the witch that is closest to you."

I couldn't help it, maybe it was the time I spent with my

father, but I started laughing. Everyone stopped eating and was staring at my small outburst.

"Ivy, are you sure you want to know more about me? I can certainly show you. Just give me your hand." I started to get up.

"Angelic, don't," Gerard warned.

I continued though, I felt bold, she pissed me off for the last time. I stretched out my hand. "Come on, or are you not as brave as you keep showing off?"

Gerard was about to get up, but Ivy got up first and stretched out her hand. I immediately grabbed it and started showing her images of the things my father had put me through. All those torturous times. She actually started screaming. Before I even knew what had happened, I was being pinned to the wall by my throat. Gerard was glaring at me, almost challenging me to do something, anything.

"I should have never come to this damn dinner, let me go, Gerard."

"You're telling me what to do? That's not the way it works, remember." He leaned in next to my ear. "I get it, you're angry and tired. Go to my room and do not leave until I come to get you." He pulled back, and I desperately wanted to challenge him, I was in a very dark mood. Once he backed off, I stormed out.

Either I gave off a very bad aura or everyone was at dinner, no one was in the hallways all the way to his bedroom. I needed to get some air. His window was already partly opened letting in the cool air. The cool ledge was an accepting chill. I had gotten so hot and angry. I might even regret what I did to her. I can't take it back though, what is done is done.

The breeze continued to softly cool me down, I felt my anger subside. Being down there may have felt shorter than three weeks, but the fact is, it was three weeks. Nothing but argues, and tests. I felt my eyes getting heavier until there was nothing but darkness.

When I woke up, I felt a soft blanket, with warm sheets. It

wasn't the windowsill I had fallen asleep on. The bed was quite large and comfortable, which could only mean one thing, Gerard put me in his bed. I could hear the rattling of papers, with an awfully slow sigh every so often. Whatever he was doing, was bothering him immensely.

I pulled myself up to look at him. "I am sorry, I don't know what has come over me. I hope Ivy is not too upset and she is feeling well."

"She had quite the scare, but more importantly when she shared to the table the images, what she saw I knew they were not meant for her eyes. It is what your father made you watch, wasn't it?" He now looked back at me. He genuinely looked concerned for me.

I had to look away, I should not have shown her those things. "He made me watch so many things, those were only a glimpse."

Gerard stood and came over to the bed, sitting next to me. His shirt was loose, and he was wearing baggy pants, possibly his sleepwear.

"I'm sorry if I took your bed, I'll head home now."

I started to get out of the bed on the opposite side but instead, I felt an arm wrap around me, pulling me back on the bed. He held my wrists down over my head, mounting over top of me. His touch was creating electricity coursing through my body. I felt the shock spark from my hands.

"You need to let it out. You're holding a lot in."

He came down close to my neck, then I felt a tug on the collar being pulled off. My fists balled. I could feel his breath along my neck. When his lips curled around my skin, I felt more electricity pulse out, he never faltered in his grip.

"Gerard, if you keep going, I might not be able to control my outbursts."

"I never asked you to, in fact, I told you to let it out."

Then I felt his teeth elongate and he bit down. He wasn't taking any blood, but he was pushing out his venom, the endorphins. My whole body arched, molding into his. The electricity shut off pulsing out into him. He gripped my wrists harder and clenched, drawing out blood, seeping down the side of my neck. He brought his hips down, pushing me into the bed. He was practically completely on top of me. He let go of my wrists and moved down to the bottom of my shirt. He placed his hands on my hip and forced me back down, then he let go of my neck.

"Does that happen every time?"

I felt it, my whole face went red, but then he just laughed and got off me, standing at the end of the bed. I had to slowly sit up, rubbing my wrists, his last hold was strong, curious how strong that electricity must have been for him to react that way.

"How are you feeling?"

I placed a hand over my neck where he had bitten me, "I suppose, better, though truthfully I am not sure what that was." He just arched an eyebrow, "I mean, it's not like that." When in fact it was, he had been the first man to ever be on top of me or make me feel that way, and those endorphins only intensified everything. I shot off the bed, "I'm not having this conversation."

"Relax, I needed you with a clear head. We will be leaving tomorrow for the desert kingdom in the morning."

"Why? What's going on?"

Gerard sighed and sat in his chair before continuing. "It is Morgan, she had gone back to her Father in the Northern Kingdom, but it appears she had disappeared. They believe she is trying to gain followers."

"Then why you? Or us?"

"The Northern territory runs above both mine and King Vern's Kingdom, if she were to take her father's place there could be war between our borders. I have no interest in having my people suffer through something so trivial."

"Then why bring me? I'm sure between the three kings she won't win."

"This is true, but why I am bringing you has nothing to do with the impending assault. Your father could return, and I would rather you be near me if he does."

"I see. Well, then I will go and pack and be ready for the morning."

"I will see you then. Oh, and Angelic," I had almost reached the door before I turned back to look at him. "Don't come for breakfast."

I smiled, "Of course." I bowed my head before leaving.

CHAPTER TWELVE

Bumping along the roads, Lucia and I were tasked with being the driver for Gerard and his men, in all, there were four carriages. I turned to look at Lucia, she was helping with pulling them along. He didn't want to risk bringing more witches than needed. Apparently, the Northern Kingdom does not exactly hate witches but treats them very differently.

I absentmindedly put my hand to my collar. He was telling me this when he had to put it back on. I also had to behave my best, otherwise, certain consequences could happen. I just had to laugh; I don't know who this king is, but he is going to have a pretty rude awakening.

"What's wrong Ava? You seem lost?"

I looked at her, and she had that damn expression of hers where you reveal all of your secrets. I sighed, "It's not that, I just keep thinking about this whole ordeal. I mean, I get why I'm coming, but why put you in danger."

"I don't mind, I wanted to come." Of course, she would.

I looked ahead and noticed we were coming up to the Desert border. We will be there by nightfall, which was good because the sun was ridiculously hot, and these vampires would need to eat sooner rather than later if they had to be exposed too long.

I turned back to Lucia, "Please try not to do anything that makes you stand out."

She burst out laughing, "You're warning me?"

Smiling back, I gave her a small nudge, "Yes, I am. You like to get into trouble, you know."

"Well then, I guess I will have to look to my teacher for an example."

I now burst into laughter. I don't care. I am so glad she is here. This trip could be dangerous, but no one will touch her.

The trip was quiet, not that many towns between the border and the king's manor. I have to admit there was more vegetation here than I remembered. Tree's were blossoming beautifully and the smaller towns we had passed were quite quaint, seemed peaceful. When we came up to the king's home, it was built like a fortress, a wall surrounding his entire manor. We came up to the guards at the front.

I knew better than to speak to them, so I just got off my seat and opened the door. Gerard stepped out. He was wearing his Royal attire with his crest on the back. The same one Lucia and I had on our collars now.

The guards bowed, "King Gerard, King Vern is expecting you. Please we will escort you and the rest of your party to him. Please have your witches bring the carriages to the West end."

Everyone got out of the rest of the carriages. Gerard turned towards us but didn't speak anything, Lucia and I just bowed and left.

This whole manor was massive, it had three levels, grand windows, built entirely of stone. It would stretch the length of a whole town, but it felt warm, soft almost. He had built it to show ruling but also welcoming. It was an odd mix.

As we came up the West end there were other carriages parked. They were a lot grander than Gerard', which almost makes me wonder if Gerard is either poor, or he doesn't care.

"What should we do now?" Lucia was looking around. There

appeared to be a guard near here, probably watching to make sure no one takes one of the carriages and runs off.

"I have no idea. Maybe just stay here? I mean I don't really have any desire to go inside. I don't recall them being very welcoming to witches. Plus it was his son that teamed up with Morgan."

"True, but didn't he punish him?"

"So he says."

We both got startled, there was a noise coming from the furthest carriage. I looked back at the guard but he didn't move. I jumped from my seat, and slowly walked up to the unknown noise, or maybe it was more of a cry?"

"Hello?" There was an instant shuffle then silence. Someone was hiding, maybe spying on us?

I waved my hand to tell Lucia to stay. Only then did I come around the corner but not to any threat, but to a petite woman with long wavy blonde hair. She was doubled over with a pile of vomit in front of her, that's when I noticed she had a very pregnant belly.

"Are you ok?"

"I'm fine, I just need to get..." She didn't move far before hurling again.

Lucia came rushing around the corner, holding the woman's hair back and grabbing her hand. The woman didn't seem to recoil at her touch.

"I am sorry." She whipped her mouth and moved to her knees, she was exhausted.

I decided to move to my knees as well to try and be less threatening. "Are you better? Do you need help to get somewhere?"

"As much as I would not want to bother you, I believe I will take you up on your offer."

Lucia grabbed one arm and I went to the other. She was quite light and easy to lift. She looked quite pale, almost sickly.

We only managed a few feet before that guard came running after us.

"Halt! Unhand her, you have no right to touch her."

Lucia and I looked at each other but I let her respond since my response would be a little too unmannered.

"Please, she needs to get to bed, she is quite ill."

He pointed his weapon at us, which I now realized was quite a long spear. "Unhand her *witch.*"

I had almost snapped before the mysterious woman spoke up, "It's fine they are only helping me to my champers. I wish for them to stay with me. You may go back to your post."

"Your highness, are you sure?"

She looked at him with a gaze that would even make me back away. "I do not need to repeat myself. The guard bowed then turned away. "I'm sorry, please just through those side doors."

She pointed to a smaller double door, it wasn't as grand as the entrance but beautiful with an ivy plant growing around the frame of it.

As we continued walking and her giving us directions in her soft voice I decided I didn't want to ask, it was obvious that she was either queen or princess, and I don't think I want to know which.

There was a large door with light flickering, I could hear men speaking. We were going to pass their meeting, and their door was wide open. I sneaked a peek at Lucia, and she had a scared look on her face, she knew who we had and what could possibly happen. Her highness was barely moving her feet, her head hung low, she was going to pass out soon.

We started to pass the doors, and before I could blink, I was pinned against the wall with a sword to my throat. Lucia was just on the other side of me.

"What's the meaning of this?" A large burly man came out. Dark brown hair with a styled beard. He knelt beside her, picking up her face slightly. She had fallen to her knees when we let her go.

I placed my hands up, which was a bad idea, the sword only pressed tighter.

"Please stop, we were helping her. She was vomiting out by the carriages and wanted us to help her to her chambers." Lucia pleaded.

Gerard was stepping out of the room with a few other men following behind. This whole scene was confusing and annoying.

I spoke out loud before I even realized it, "Now I get it, she's pregnant with a shifter, that's tough."

King Vern was in front of me in a flash, the sword was gone, and his hand was wrapped around my throat. Shifters may not be as fast as vampires, but they are still extremely fast.

"What did you say, witch?" It practically came out as a growl.

"King Vern, please don't hurt my property." He looked towards me. "Angelic explain."

The king loosened his grip but didn't let go. "She is pregnant in this home, so I can only assume it is from another shifter, yes?" He didn't do anything except his gaze became more threatening. "I am just saying it looks as though she may be giving birth within the next few days, but she is becoming ill. If she were a shifter this would be fine, but as she is not, she could possibly not survive the birthing."

I felt the movement of him squeezing, he was going to have my head, but in an instant, Gerard was standing in front of me with King Vern's hand pulled away.

"As I said, don't hurt my property."

"She is threatening my son's wife!"

"She is not threatening, only stating what is happening."

"I can help her!" Lucia practically screamed it, and it worked. Everyone had eyes on her. "I know the medicine that can help, it can help her stop vomiting, hopefully, help her eat some food. I also know some remedies that can help the birthing process, at least make it a little easier on the mother." She was slightly trembling, but she was holding up well.

Gerard turned back to Vern, "She has skill in her herbs and remedies, I have even taken aid to them."

"Alright, Gerard, if you think your witches can help, then do so."

We didn't need an order to start moving. Once Lucia was let go, we both got back to her and helped her up. We bowed our heads then continued towards her chambers. Everyone was back inside, and the door slammed shut before we even made it down the hall.

Her room wasn't that much further, up some stairs and to the left. Her room was gorgeous, filled with the softest bedding, a grand balcony, and the smell of lavender. We placed her on the bed before we all completely toppled over. Her temperature had increased, and she was breathing pretty heavily.

"Ava, can you go into the bathroom and find a cloth, make sure it is cool."

I immediately went to the side bathroom. A long-stretched mirror with two sinks, and a deep tub. On the other end, I saw purple and black towels. Warming a small cloth up I returned to Lucia.

"Just place it on her forehead." I did as I was told. She really looked uncomfortable.

"What now?"

Lucia placed her hands on the girls' stomach. "The baby is still moving, so it is probably still healthy, but this illness is draining everything she has." Lucia looked up to me, "She needs to get better or she won't survive."

I swallowed what little saliva I had, We couldn't let her die. "I wonder what her name is."

"Lilac."

We both looked over to the door to see a tall lean man leaning on the door. He was the same one that was holding Lucia down in the hallway.

"Sorry to intrude, how is she?" He came over to the side of the bed, it took Lucia a second to break her gaze from him.

"I need to get some supplies, she needs certain herbs, but she also needs to be able to drink it."

"Well, I can take you to the kitchen if you think you can find what you need there."

Lucia stared at him for a moment before she could respond. "Yes, thank you. Ava, can you watch Lilac?"

"Of course."

"Please follow me, the name is Erik by the way."

"Pleased to meet you." She did a small bow. "My name is Lucia, and this is Angelic." I smiled and nodded my head at him.

They both left the room, closing the door behind them. Lilac sounded strong but yet she got sick. Looking around a bit more she had small trinkets everywhere, it was either dried flowers, small rocks, letters.

The door burst open before I could keep looking around. Another male came in, he was a bit shorter than Eric, but same color hair, and eyes. He looked at me for a moment but went straight to Lilac.

"Tell me, witch, is she going to be alright? Did we make a mistake thinking that a human could survive?" He never looked at me but was holding her hand staring intently at her face.

I looked over to see another woman, gowned in a lady's maid uniform. She was another petite woman with short blond hair.

"Was she like this the whole pregnancy?"

He sighed before answering but looked my way. "No, she was happy and healthy. She was still riding the horses even."

"When did you notice her appetite change? Or when she started to vomit?"

"I would say maybe ten days ago. She started to tell me her belly hurt at night. Sarah," He nodded to the other women, "Was able to make up some remedies that helped for a little while, but Lilac had only kept getting worse."

Very peculiar, "I am sure Lucia will come back with something that could help her sleep, then in the morning hopefully she will be awake long enough so we can get some food for her. She did say the baby felt fine though."

He smiled down at his wife, then kissed the top of her belly. He seemed like a very gentle man, for a werewolf. They both seemed very different compared to our encounter in the hallway.

"Ryker!"

"Erik, thank you for helping us."

"Of course, brother, but I had thought you were going to Cedar to find medicine?"

"I had caught wind that she was getting worse. I wouldn't be able to live with myself if I was not here during her greatest time of need."

Lucia broke in between them, "I'm sure I can help. Just help me get her into a sitting position."

Lucia took a bowl full of herbs and cast a small flame. Once it started burning, she blew out the flame and put it under Lilac's nose.

"This will help her sleep hopefully for a full day."

Ryker placed her back down in bed and gave her a small kiss on her forehead. "Thank you."

"Ryker, we need to tell father you are home. He will want you to join us, maybe we can convince him to let you stay."

"He would never go for that, you know that."

"Ryker, you are one of our strongest, if anyone could help stop Morgan it would be you." That is the first time the Sarah lady had spoken up. Quite the high-pitched, eery voice, and who would want the father to leave the mother and child?

"Thank you, Sarah, I will go talk to my father about what we should do."

"I will come with you brother." He turned to Lucia, "Please take care of her."

"I will." Lucia tried to give a reassuring smile.

Once they were gone, Lucia turned to me. "What are you thinking Ava?"

"Huh?"

"You have that look."

"I'm sorry," I tried to give her all my attention. "I think you should go and get some rest. Lilac will need you when she wakes."

"What will you do?"

"I'm going to watch Lilac."

"I can do that!" Sarah spoke out. She was still here.

"I think you should go help Ryker. You two seem to know each other."

For a moment I saw a grin, "Yes, I think that would be best for me as well. I am sure I can ease his mind."

"Thank you, Sarah." She finally left. "You too, leave. I will be fine looking after her."

"Alright, but don't go doing anything. You know what will happen if you use any healing magic on her."

"Yes, now go." I practically pushed her out the door, slamming it behind her.

Turning back to Lilac, she was right, magic would save her life, but to a newborn shifter, it could kill him.

I smell betrayal here, her being completely healthy, then magically becomes ill before her due date. I took a seat in the darkest corner, placing a shadow over me, it's the same I used when Gerard first met me. It was a long wait, but I had to be sure.

The night turned to day, and my shadow remained. Some people had come and gone. Ryker was here a lot, so was his brother. Lilac still slept right into nightfall. I was getting hungry and was starting to doubt myself when the door finally crept open slowly. Load and behold Sarah was coming in.

She didn't take her time; she pulled a small glass vile from her sleeve. She started to head over next to Lilac and tried to lift her head. Whatever it was, she was going to make her drink it. Luckily the vines had just reached her leg causing her to jump backwards.

She was screaming, I quickly moved to cover her mouth. The vines were completely wrapped around her, immobilizing her.

"Now, how obvious could you have made this." Her eyes went wide. "I mean wanting him to leave for the birth, immediately jumping on the opportunity to be by his side. Maybe to those close to you, it may not have been obvious, but to an outsider, it was all too easy to see." I removed my hand from her mouth and stepped back.

"You witch, this is going to help her. I figured I could give it to her so that she could take Lucia's medicine."

"You know, I hate liars." I squeezed the vines harder, causing her to scream.

The door slammed open, piling in practically everyone. Ryker was on me in an instant, I didn't bother trying to protect myself.

"What is the meaning of this?"

Sarah was able to pull away from the vines and went straight to Ryker's side. "She tried to kill me!"

"Is this a true witch?" Ryker's grip became tighter, and his gaze narrowed.

CHAPTER THIRTEEN

"Angelic," Gerard came in behind everyone.

"Would you people just wait; she takes longer than all you."

Just then I heard Lucia making her way down the hall, her feet slamming against the floor.

"Angelic, what's going on?" She was huffing pretty good, she must have been skipping three steps at a time.

"Lucia, I need you to take the vial, tell me, is it actually safe?" Rykers gripped weakened until he finally let me go.

"It's too late I dropped it when you startled me." She was very smug.

I waved my hand and Ivy brought out the little vial wrapped safely in its leaf. I put it right in front of Lucia. Once she grabbed it and opened it; her face shifted. I was right.

"It's poison."

"Are you sure?" Erik spoke, as he placed his hand on Lucia's shoulder.

"With certainty, but I also know what she needs now." She looked up to Erik, "Can you take me to the kitchen again?"

His smile reached his eyes, "Definitely," he turned to his brother, "She is going to be alright."

They nodded at each other before Lucia and he had left. Ryker immediately had his hands gripped around Sarah.

She started to scream, "No! It should have been me! Ryker you love me." She was pleading, almost crying.

"I told you when we had our time, that it was never permanent." Ryker's eyes began to glow, and his irises turned to gold.

Vern took Ryker's shoulder, "She will go to the dungeon, killing her now won't do any good."

Through gritted teeth, he agreed. He pulled Sarah's arm behind her back forcing her to walk out of the room. King Vern followed behind nodding at Gerard, like they had an agreement.

"You just can't stay out of trouble can you."

"I did just save her life."

Gerard moved in front of me. His light touch lifted my chin to meet his gaze. "Indeed." He kissed me, then started to trail down to my chin, then further down to my neck. He must have been hungry, his soft kisses turned into a sharp pinch. I needed to grab onto the front of his shirt just to keep balanced, and grounded. Once he was done, I felt his tongue slide across the wound, then he took a step back.

"How did my hard work turn into your reward?"

He gave a smug look, "You didn't enjoy that?"

Damn him. Lilac was starting to stir just a little, she would finally wake up, everything would be ok. My sigh came out a lot more audible than I thought it would have.

"We had a suspicion you were up to something but during breakfast, Lucia told us to just hold out. I'm sure everyone will gladly accept you now."

"I wasn't really looking for acceptance, but I'll take it." I smiled up at him, maybe over time, I can change the way the world sees witches.

Lucia came in with another bowl of herbs floating in water. "Sorry, did I interrupt?"

Gerard spoke first, "Continue what you were doing, if you need anything just let any one of us know. And you," He turned to me again, "Go get food and get some sleep. We will be leaving tomorrow night." He then silently left the room, leaving me with a lightweight feeling.

"I can handle this, and he is right, you need food and rest."

Right then my stomach growled. "Ha, yeah I'll let you handle things from here, but if you need me, call."

I turned to leave the room, closing the door behind me. It was quiet. I also had no idea where I was going. I made a right then went down the stairs. Erik and Ryker seemed to be discussing something at the entrance. Before I could hear anything, they turned to me.

"Hello, any chance you know where I could get some food."

Ryker smiled, "I will take you. I need to thank you for what you have done." Ryker placed his hand on my back and started leading me down the hall. "Erik, we will talk later." If Erik replied I wouldn't know, he had already taken me down another hallway.

"I have to thank you for what you did. I didn't think I would ever get her back."

"You're welcome." I didn't know what to say.

We made it to the kitchen pretty quickly, when he opened the doors there was an abundance of smells coming from every-where. Some were chopping vegetables, there were things brewing over a fire, and the number of people working in sequence was amazing.

"Molly!" Ryker yelled out to the room. A short woman with short brown hair came up our way.

"Yes, Prince Ryker?" She gave a small curtsy on her greeting.

"This is Angelic, she needs food, possibly a lot of it. Could you take care of that for us?"

"Of course." The lady smiled at me then grabbed my arm. "Please come with me."

I was hesitant at first, but Ryker gave me a small nudge and I followed her through the kitchen. I couldn't help noticing that everyone seemed genuinely happy. I'm not sure what happened here in the Desert Kingdom, but it is in no way of what I remember.

"Just wait here and I will get you a plate."

"Thank you." She quickly left me standing at the edge of a counter. There was another door just beside me and I could hear the small sounds of conversation wafting in.

"Here you are."

She placed a significantly large portion of food in front of me. "I'm sorry but what is it?"

She gave a good laugh, "If you don't know what this is then I feel sorry for you. It's called spaghetti."

"Spa-ghe-tti," it smelled amazing, all the herbs and tomato sauce being brought together.

"Please follow me."

I grabbed my plate and followed her out through the doors. I was right, it was a dining room. There seemed to still be quite a few people eating. It was also refreshing to see shifters and humans eating together so casually, maybe one day witches as well.

"Here you are." She pulled out a small chair for me at a round table by a door. I could only assume that it would lead outside since there were windows on the same wall. "Well, I will let you enjoy it, if you need anything let me know." She quickly turned and walked back to the kitchen.

The table had utensils and water laid out. The spaghetti was hard to maneuver on my fork, but eventually, I was able to take a bite. I had to admit this may become my new favorite dish. It had everything one could ask for, a flavorful mixture of herbs and vegetables all coming together.

It didn't take me long to finish, and it was completely filling. I grabbed a glass of water and just watched the crowd around me. They seemed to be talking about their day. I knew that the king had to be up during the night to make it easier on Gerard and his men.

I quickly pulled away from my table and snuck through the

door. It had led out to a small garden patch. Quickly running through the laid-out stone path I was able to reach a stretched-out piece of land with green grass and a few trees. There weren't many with large shade, but I found an older one that seemed to do the trick.

Settling next to the tree, it was more feminine, she felt thoroughly happy that someone was settling at her trunk, asking for shade. I found a nice flat, smooth spot. It would be perfect until nightfall, or whenever I woke up. Once I rested my head on my arm, with my full stomach, and not sleeping for almost two days, I fell asleep in an instant.

There was a slight nudge on my shoulder. It startled me awake, I shot up to a sitting position to see a smiling, light brown eyed girl staring at me.

"Lilac! I'm sorry you startled me."

"Sorry, I saw you laying here and just needed to talk to you before they came to get you."

"Oh?" Looking around the sun was setting, casting long shadows.

She then embraced me into a hug, nearly knocking me over. I had to use one of my arms just to hold us up.

"Thank you so much!" Her voice was shaky. "If you ever need anything, please ask me. I owe you everything." She was starting to cry, and I placed both my hands around her. These two were so similar I can see why they fell in love.

Someone cleared their throat behind us, looking up at Ryker. Lilac let me go before moving away, going to stand next to him. She gave him a light kiss on the cheek before she went back inside.

"We need to go."

I stood up slowly, giving a small thanks for the shade and protection I left with Ryker. I followed him to the front of the manor. It was filled with men and women talking and bickering. They were all coming with us to the Northern Kingdom. Gerard men stood off to the side, and he and Vern were at the front, along with Erik. Ryker went to his father and I went to Gerard.

"How is this going to work? We couldn't possibly make it using carriages."

"No, we will be running this time."

I choked on the breath I was taking, "What?" I looked back around, and I could see some of the shifters already changing. There were a few vampires among them but not many. I wasn't allowed to transform into my own shadow wolf form because he didn't want them to know about me. "If I calculate this right it should take me a month?"

Gerard just chuckled before coming close. He quickly scooped me up in his arms, cradling me in front of him. Oh dear, my cheeks flushed.

"Gerard, this is a little atypical of you."

"Just be sure to keep your head against me."

He turned to King Vern and nodded.

Vern turned to his men, "Alright everyone you know the plan and route. Head out!" Immediately the rest shifted. I saw Ryker turn into a massive black wolf, that explains the black towels. His brother, beside him, was a massive white wolf, what a funny pair.

Gerard turned to his men and just moved his head slightly, and they were off. Everyone was gone in a flash. I immediately grabbed Gerard's shirt and pulled my head into his chest. Instantly I felt air pushing me against him. I could only imagine I was slowing him down. Getting this close to him again I could smell him, he smelt so nice, it relaxed me quite a bit. I felt a small rumble in his chest, I felt my face turn red, oh man I totally said that out loud. Sighing and relaxing into Gerard I decided to shut my eyes and just wait until it was over.

When we stopped, I felt Gerard's arms tighten around me and my body wanted to fling forward. He let me stand, it took me a minute to find my footing, but he didn't seem to mind me using him as a balancing post.

Everyone started to appear around us, so he was fastest even with me. Looking around I could see we were no longer in a peaceful area. This place was dark, the clouds rumbled above us with no rain. The mountains were behind us and the land ahead of us was rock and decay.

"Angelic," I turned back to Gerard. He passed me his cloak that he had worn when we first arrived at Vern's manor. "Keep this on and the hood up, and at all costs don't look up." He flung it around my shoulders and buttoned up the front. It was so unusual I was stunned into stillness.

Vern spoke up, "You can stay with Erik and Ryker. They will keep you between themselves."

I looked back at them; Erik had his usual grin with his arm outstretched. "My lady, if you please." I smiled and took my place between them but just behind by a step or two.

Everyone else stayed up in the mountain and we made our way down the crater. It was a slippery road, they had to catch me a couple of times. Unless you have quick reflexes, this place could kill you before you reach it.

When we reached our destination, I couldn't help but look up, this was a castle, I almost questioned myself if I was heading in to see my father or not.

"Ava, head down." Ryker whispered.

I pulled the hood taught and put my eyes to the ground. Not that I actually needed them to be able to maneuver myself. We continued in and I could hear the doors swing open.

"Welcome and please follow me." Whoever this was, it was a witch, I could feel her power. So he had witches as slaves, if I don't end up murdering this king myself, it would be a miracle.

I followed behind them with ease, their energy was easy to follow. Shifters had an incredibly soft and warm feeling, compared to vampires who give off a void of space that just felt cold. The floor was stone, and a few times I had seen rats scurrying along. The instant we made it to the throne room I knew. This King gave off an energy that could kill.

"King Cain, it is a pleasure to see you again." Vern had spoken out first.

I heard him get off his throne, stepping down some stairs, but instead of welcoming Vern he moved to the witch.

"I do not believe I gave you permission to enter this room."

Fear, there was so much fear coming from her it was almost over bearing. I felt a hand grab my arm. They knew I would move the instant I heard it. He slapped her.

"Get yourself back downstairs. You don't need to be here." I felt the air of her running out the door when she passed. "King Vern, welcome I am so glad you could be here.".

"Yes, well you seemed quite distraught when you called for us."

"Yes, my daughter seems to keep increasing her followers. I hear she is even going to other Kingdoms to increase her numbers."

"Yes, and if we see any of our people in this assault they will be treated as traitors just like the others."

"Indeed," His voice seemed to trail off, then Erik and Ryker backed away. I remained still. "What is this?"

"She belongs to me, Cain." Gerard spoke.

"You bring your witch here?"

"She is useful."

"I will be the judge of that." I felt the hood pulled back, it was pushed back that it was pressing on my neck, then I got a good look at him. He was paler than any vampire, with almost black eyes, he stood lean and lithe, with his black hair to add to his entire contrast color. He continued to stare at my eyes before he spoke, "I have to admit she has quite an empowering feeling. Her hair length shows she has been hiding for some time, she must be new to you." He continued to walk around me, "Her stand is proud, I could only imagine you would need to fight her for any commands."

Gerard took a few steps forward, stopping Cain in his place, "She is loyal to me, if I ask her to do something then she will."

"Oh, I would like to see that, they kind of seem to never get anything right."

Gerard sighed, "And what is it you want?"

"Hmmm," he lightly tapped his finger on his chin before he grinned. "It does get quite cold here, why doesn't she warm up the place."

What does that even mean, does he want a small warming fire, an engulfing flame, or just the air to be warmed up. Gerard nodded at me, how annoying but I went with the latter. I stepped back from him a bit before focusing on the air in the room. I gave it some heat, causing the room to warm up. It is actually quite difficult then just creating a flame.

"How is she making it warm with no flame?"

"As I said, she is useful."

Cain's gaze tightened, "That may be, but she will need to be placed downstairs with the rest."

One of his guards came forward, "Take her downstairs, then the rest of us will get to the details of my daughter's little defiance."

The guard grabbed my arm and started dragging me out. I heard them move together and started conversing with each other before I was out of the room. As we made our way, I was able to get a better look. It was just as dark and damp as it felt, and looked like a dungeon, so I could only imagine what down-stairs would look like.

There was a small door that had tight twirling stairs. He pushed me ahead and I continued down. I was pretty surprised to see what was here, it was a gigantic room with many witches. There were a few beds, but not enough for everyone. There were also a couple fires that many of them huddled too. The guard marched back out, heading up the stairs, I would assume that door would be locked.

Walking through the room, only a few looked up, there had to be at least a hundred of us here. It wasn't long before I found the girl, she was next to a few others who were trying to console her.

"Hey, are you okay?" Everyone looked back, and one male in particular had determined eyes, he was the strongest one here.

"Elle, will you be alright staying here with the others?" Through her tears she nodded.

He stood and came towering over me, "I'm sorry, she is new and trying to figure out how to live here. It's hard to adjust too."

"I would imagine." They were shivering. "Why aren't there more fires?"

"Sadly, I can only make a couple, and it's first come first serve down here."

"That's sad." I swung my hand out, creating a blaze large enough for them, along with a couple more around the room.

There was a quick commotion of scrambling, but everyone was enjoying the warmth. It put a smile on my face, they needed help and I was determined now to help them.

"These are amazing, you are a strong witch."

I smiled back at him, "Something like that."

"Please," he outstretched his arm towards Elle and the other group.

I sat with my back to the wall, enjoying the warmth the fire gave. I wouldn't be able to keep them around forever but hopefully long enough for them to have some enjoyment.

"What's your name?" Elle asked.

"Angelic," She smiled, god she looked younger than I thought. "How old are you Elle?"

"Fifteen," she almost seemed confused by my question, like it was obvious.

"I'll kill him." It slipped out, this man was hurting fifteen-year olds, there still kids.

"Haha, that would be quite the feat, but if you did that you would have your own master coming after you."

"What do you mean?"

"The Kings are required to help each other. It's part of their treaty, they have to come if any one of them is called upon by the other."

"I didn't know that."

"It's not common knowledge for commoners. I just happened to be in the same room when they talked about it."

I felt a head hit my side, Elle fell asleep, falling on top of me. I left her there, I wonder what happened to her family. Or to any one of their families. Looking around the room they all seemed alone.

"It wasn't always like this." I turned my attention back to him. "A witch killed the king's wife. Since then he has never been the same." That makes sense, but to treat everyone like this because of one bad witch.

I let my head hit the back wall. This had to change, I would have to think of something, even if that meant having to battle all the Kings, even Gerard.

CHAPTER FOURTEEN

Two guards came barreling in. They were running right for us. "River! River!" The man across from me stirred, so that was his name. "The King requires you immediately. It's Osran, he's been injured." The shock that came across his face worried me. Whoever Osran was, he was very important to River.

River stood quickly sprinting out with the guards, and since no one was watching I followed behind. They were hard to keep up with, but I was able to keep them in my view. We were heading back to the throne room.

When they barreled through the doors, I could see the scene inside. Cain was cradling, who I could only assume was Ocean's head in his lap. He was in a lot of pain, shifting and squirming in Cain's hold. The others were standing near watching the scene.

"River! heal him, quick!" Cain was commanding, screaming at him.

River kneeled beside them, but he went into total shock.

"What is wrong with you River! This is obviously magic, heal him from it!" River didn't move.

I spoke first, "It's a curse." I walked up calmly to them. "He will die." River flinched on my words; he was trying to hold back his tears.

"Ava, are you sure?" Gerard asked.

"Not even the slightest doubt."

"My wife, now my son! I will kill all of you!" Cain was about to move but Gerard got in front of him first.

"Angelic, can you heal him with your other abilities?" I knew he would ask, maybe this was part of that treaty River was talking about.

"I can, but I won't unless you order me too."

"Angelic, I am ordering you to help him. Do not let him die."

I sighed, "Damn. You all need to get away from him."

"Gerard, what is she..."

"Cain move." It took him a moment, but he gently let Osran's head on the floor and moved back, River followed back with him.

I watched him squirming on the floor. He was clutching at his throat, which makes me think they made him swallow this curse. I hated this, I don't want to have to do this, curses are some of the darkest magic my father had put on the surface.

I knelt and started to shift until I was in my wolf form. I don't look like a typical wolf. My fur would flicker in the light, just like a shadow would. Everyone moved back a step, they knew what I was now, which world I belonged to.

I stepped towards Osran stepping over top of him. I bared my teeth, growling, it was what I expected, a mouse was eating at his artery, forcing a permanent hole. Even with his vampire healing it would continue until Osran ran out of energy and couldn't heal anymore. The mouse stirred, even flicked a whisker but just continued to eat. I really had hoped that would work, scare him to return home, but now I had to take control of it and there was only one way to do that.

I had to grow for this to work. My form became larger than any of the shifters that were here. I growled one last time before my teeth came barreling down on Ocean's throat. To others it would look like I'm attacking him, but there is only one thing that I'm going after.

Everything seemed to happen at once, everyone was reaching for me, but I pulled back before they could, dragging the damn mouse with me. I didn't want to look at them. This was the worst part. I chewed it, swallowing the curse, forcing it to be mine. It burned so bad. I returned back to my human form. I couldn't get up, staying on all fours I was going to hurl.

I wasn't sure who spoke my name, everything was muffled.

"Stay back!" Oh god, talking burned. I clenched my eyes shut.

Then it came, the black molasses, it was thick and grimy. It took a couple tries but it all came out. It formed back into its original form, a shade. This one was a small boy, he turned to me with his blackened pupils, and short cut hair. He was even more poised than Gerard.

"What is this, who is that!" Cain was screaming at me.

I stood up, holding my stomach, this always left me queasy and weak. I looked back at the boy, he bore a bored look. His eyes shifted to behind me.

I turned back to them, "I told you to stay back!" River was helping Osran up, and the others stood still. No one had seen the true forms of curses; they would kill the user if they had.

"Your services are no longer required. Go home with the others." I couldn't look at it, I couldn't treat it like anything other than what it was.

"But mum, they will hurt you." He came up beside me, he was staring at the energy they were giving off. They indeed had killer intentions, and he could sense it.

I closed my eyes, and sighed heavily, "They won't hurt me. Besides, they couldn't if they tried." He still had a bored facial expression. He truly is a strong curse, maybe my strongest. I had been hunting them until I thought there were no more left.

I gave off the most powerful gaze I could back at everyone. I had to stand straight, I had to make them back off. I felt the boy's eyes shift to me.

When he looked away, he went straight to Gerard, "Who is he mum? He is like you and Grandpa, but not?" Shit my blood is all Gerard had now, of course he would notice it.

Gerard moved in front of him, returning the boy's gaze and poise back at it. "When she is here, she belongs to me."

The boy looked him up and down. "You are strong." The boy bowed, if I didn't see it, I wouldn't believe it. He just gave his loyalty to Gerard. "I will leave you now mum, father." He then molded into the ground, returning to the Shadow Realm.

Nobody moved, everyone was too stunned by it, so naturally I spoke first, "Congratulations, you now have the loyalty of a curse." The pain in my stomach started up again forcing me back down to my knees. I couldn't hurl again, that was just embarrassing.

Cain spoke, "Gerard, what is the meaning of this? Who is she?"

"Isn't it obvious father, the Shadow King had a child." I looked up to Osran. He was smiling, staring down with his piercing blue eyes, his ashen hair was a mess from his ordeal. "And you," he turned to Gerard, "You somehow have control over her."

Ryker spoke first, "Settle Osran, we don't know anything right now. She could be playing Gerard for all we know."

"I wouldn't have bothered to save your wife if I was." I stumbled my way back to a standing position." I turned my gaze to Osran, "And this did not come without a cost from you."

Cain came out of his daze now, "You don't make orders here, you are still a witch, that means you serve us."

"It's fine, she did save my life, and from what I see, it came at a worse price to her than whatever I could give back. Tell me what your price is?"

I looked towards River, "For you to listen to River, on his advice you will change your policies of your treatment towards witches. They will no longer be treated like scum," I stood up as straight as I could, "Or I will challenge all of you." I looked at each King, resting lastly on Gerard.

"Done."

"Osran you do not make the commands here."

Osran turned towards his father, "I will take the throne by force if you try to stop this from happening." His gaze was like ice, you would freeze just gazing upon it.

"Hump." He stormed off towards a long table in the back of the room. They must have been making their strategy, maps were sprawled out everywhere.

"River!" He marched over in front of Osran. "Go to the kitchen, tell them to make a feast for everyone downstairs."

The river was grinning from ear to ear. "Yes, my Lord." He bowed then quickly ran out of the room. Oh good, it didn't take as long as I thought it would to fix that problem.

I felt myself falling forward, black spots were covering my vision, but before I fell, I was scooped up into a pair of arms. He carried me out of this room, I turned in-wards taking in his sweet and musky scent.

"So, you would turn against me."

"No, you would turn against them." I felt the rumble in his chest.

I was in and out of consciousness, I felt him laying me on a bed with others surrounding it. Their voices were just muffled now. I couldn't stay awake anymore, I fell back into a deep sleep.

I shot up in the bed, only to be greeted by a wave of dizziness. It took me a minute, but everything was coming back into focus. I was downstairs in King Cain's basement, where he places all of them. When I looked around though there was no one here, I heard footsteps coming down the stairs.

"Good morning," River was smiling with a plate of food in his hands.

"Good morning?" It came out as more of a question, than a greeting.

"Yes, you were asleep for a while." He sat on the edge of the bed placing a plate of fruit and eggs in front of me. I dug in immediately.

"Can you tell me what is going on? Where is everyone?"

"Well after the feast Osran told anyone who wants to go can go, and anyone that wants to help can stay. There are a few of us now, I think we will be enough to change things."

I placed my hand over his, "You are enough." I tried to put on my best smile, but truthfully my worry was going to explode out.

"Anyways, you've been asleep for two days. I suppose you would be quite hungry after that."

There is no way, "Two Days!" I shot out of the bed but before I could run out he grabbed my arm.

"It's too late, they're gone." Damn it Gerard.

I went to the side of the bed and grabbed my cloak. "Where were they heading?"

"Angelic, they can handle it."

"Do you not remember they were able to place a curse on Osran, or did you forget what that means?"

"Calamity witch." I nodded in agreement. Morgan found something or someone that had a lot of power. That curse was strong, so it had to be someone stronger than a normal class 5.

"I have to go." He let go of my arm.

"They left for the Eastern mountains, they're called Eternal Tomb. It's not the easiest place to get to but if you keep heading East I'm sure you'll find your way."

I grabbed his hand and gave it a squeeze. "It will be alright, I promise; I'll look after Osran, he seems like he would be a better suited King here."

He lightly squeezed my hand back. "Thank you, Angelic, you changed things here forever, we will never forget, and hope you will visit after everything."

"Of course, I have to make sure he keeps up with his promise." I let him go and started heading to the door. "See you around River." Then I bolted out running to the entrance.

It wasn't hard to find, but outside had definitely become darker, and he was right it won't be hard to find, just follow the darkest clouds in the East. It was almost comical how obvious it was; but I also couldn't take my time, they may have been fighting by now. I returned to my wolf form, and with an immensely powerful force I lunged towards them. I just hoped they could hold out until I got there.

I reached what I believe was the Eternal Tomb. It was a Valley in the middle of towering mountains; but getting down there could be difficult, there seemed to be paths all over the place with discarded bones. I had to walk in different directions trying to get a better view of the Valley. The rocks were sharp causing me to cut myself a few times and tearing my cloak.

I ended up reaching a spot that looked to be an overhang. Peering over I saw them, all of them. I was right they were fighting, and Morgan had gained a massive number of followers. I found Gerard pretty quick, besides looking a bit dirty he seemed fine.

"Quite the scene, don't you think." I didn't turn.

"It's not surprising I suppose."

"Why do you dwell on the surface problems? You could come home and not deal with any of this."

I now turned to face him, "Those lines are getting old." I didn't want to deal with him right now. "Father, if you don't leave you will get caught in the cross-hairs, and I know how much you hate dealing with us up here." Lightning was starting to charge off me.

"Kill her Slain!" I turned to see Morgan. She was in battle armor and panting pretty hard. She even had slashes all over her body, one was even across her neck.

"So that's the name you picked this time."

"I needed to use something that would be better than Shadow King." He just gradually shrugged.

Morgan stumbled back, "Shadow King." She was able to

compose herself before she completely lost it though. "You said you work for me now. I'm ordering you to kill her."

My father was about to raise his hands, killing her in flames I'm sure, but Gerard got in the way, protecting her. My father got his annoying amused grin back.

"Oh Gerard, I so missed you; are you leaving my dear Angelic and going back to her?" He turned back to me, "See daughter he doesn't want you, come home."

He's completely back to playing his games. He couldn't take a single thing seriously. Maybe that's what happens when you have been living as long as him, you go completely insane.

Gerard walked away from Morgan and right up to me, "Why did you come, you should be resting."

"No, I'm the one who's pissed for being left behind!" He just stood there, giving me his dominant stance. Stubborn bastard.

"Here's a fun thought, maybe he thought you had worked hard enough." My father was grinning. "I met him, nice boy, how you survived his second birth is beyond me." My father casually shook his head in a mocking manner.

Gerard didn't take the news of me possibly dying very well. He was gone in a flash, almost hitting him, but he grabbed Gerard's fist before impact. Gerard just maneuvered to go for another hit, but he blocked it. They continued back and forth, until Gerard finally backed away.

"Here is something else that could be fun. Why don't you take control of my creatures? That would stop the war pretty quickly." He was so amused with himself.

Morgan spoke up, "You are supposed to be..." She started screaming, black flames engulfed her.

"Dear, I work for no one." She was gone. He may have just sent her somewhere, but he wouldn't tell us even if we asked. She had irritated him. "Now, come on Gerard, end this war."

I attacked my father with the lightning I was charging. It would have been a strong hit, but he reverberated it back. He didn't attack me with it, but it shot out over the Valley. I had his attention now.

"You keep saying I am you; I belong to you, I am your daughter; but you know what, it takes two." I returned his grin; the clouds were charged, and this would be a hit that even he couldn't avoid.

When the clouds came raining down with lightning, it hit in multiple locations. He was evading though, I needed to use more power. I felt the shift, this wasn't like anything I had ever tried before. I could feel it rising, pulsating out, the force would knock back anyone who got close enough.

"Taking on your mothers looks now, the very pretty eyes she had. Shimmering pink, bordering on red, you know..." He stumbled his words, he never faltered, but instead he started to look more sinister. "You may want to be your mother, but you will never be able to get away from me."

He created a mirror and I saw it, one eye was a vibrant pink, but the other was as black as charcoal. I created a flame but it was a black flame with a pinkish reflection. He was right, even now I can feel his power more than my mothers.

My father said, "Well, if Gerard here won't do it, then I will."

The shadows started to move from every tree, rock, and person. It moved to the ground, and over the ledge. I ran to look over and once they reached the valley they started to rise, creating the same lithe black creatures, with their long claws.

Everyone stopped moving and watched as they were being formed. Everyone seemed confused and unsure of what was happening, but then they started moving, attacking them. Everyone immediately started battling again. They at least stopped attacking each other but this foe was so much worse. As they tried to kill them more were being created. It was possible to send them back to the Shadow Realm, but once they got their strength back they could head right back up to the surface, it would be an unending fight, at least, until every living thing was dead.

I tried to reach for them, like before, but I couldn't. My fathers command was too strong.

"Stop this!" I turned back to him.

"If you want them to stop, then stop them yourself."

I looked back over the ledge, everyone seemed to be holding up well, but not all. There were some running from the field, others getting hurt from the Shadows touch. I needed to try to at least help everyone in some way. I would heal them for as long as my strength would last. I had to use so much magic to do this, my Shadow self will want to take over while it's depleted.

"You may not care about them, but I do." I stood towering over the ledge. "Good-bye" Then I jumped.

I grew wings, spreading them out, slowing my fall. They were dark against the night sky, but they were as beautiful and as swift as an owl's hunt. When I landed, I was able to knock back everyone around me, creature, and vampire alike. My Shadow blades formed in my hands, I used two at a time, they could kill them making sure that they would not return.

I had to help Ryker and Erik first. They started to get surrounded. I was able to jump and take flight right into the circle they created around them. Killing many of them until they backed away, running to other vampires.

"Not that I don't appreciate the help, but what the hell are you?" Erik was out of breath as he spoke.

"Unfortunately, nothing good." I smiled back at him, but then I felt the stabbing pain. My magic was being overused. If I kept this up, I could erupt, and my magic would burst killing every-one. Hence why were called calamity witches; or worse my Shadow self would come out, killing everything without a shred of thought. I knelt down trying to hold it in.

"Angelic! What's wrong?" Ryker was kneeling in front of me now.

"There are just a lot of you here. It takes a lot to heal everyone from the shadows' touch."

Ryker looked at his arm where one of the creatures grabbed him, it was healing quickly enough that he had barely noticed it.

"You need to stop, you will cause more damage in the end, then what it's worth."

"Don't worry, I won't let him win." I was able to stand again.

I pushed past him and started to attack them again, but I felt an arrow hit me, it pushed me back quite far. The wound around the arrowhead was bleeding black. Ryker was right, I would lose everything pretty soon.

When I came back from my short haze, I could see the creatures retreating. They started to return back home? Looking up I saw Gerard over the ledge, he was concentrating, and my father was close behind him. He did it, Gerard is controlling my father's army. He won; I couldn't protect him from my father. This also just proves I'm not stronger than Gerard, even though I couldn't take control over them.

I pulled the arrow out, healing the wound with what little strength I had left. I fell to my knees; everything was starting to turn black. I felt my form turn completely back to human and my blades returned home. I was falling forward until I hit someone. My eyes were shut but I could smell the sweet musky scent. It was the last thing I noticed before I had lost consciousness.

CHAPTER FIFTEEN

I felt short breaths hitting the side of my face, it tickled my cheek as my hair lightly touched my skin. Opening my eyes there was a small boy with black hair curled up next to me. It didn't take him long to open his eyes after me.

"You're awake." He smiled widely, this was not the same poise boy from Cain's castle.

"Yeah, what's going on?"

"You were sleeping for a long time, papa said not to bother you. He said you wouldn't wake until you were ready."

I eased my way into a sitting position. I was back in my old room. The cloak from Gerard was hanging on the side of my bed. There were also some herbs in a bowl on my nightstand, though they seemed to be old. I felt the bed shift.

"I'm going to go tell Papa you are up."

He started out of the room before I could protest. Though even if I did, I was still quite confused about what happened. I remember the battle, and my father, then Gerard; but what I had done, I thought it might have killed me. I quickly got out of bed and changed, noticing that my clothes were different from what I was last wearing. I put on a light deep green dress.

I walked through the halls slowly, I felt strong but unsteady on my feet. I don't know how long I was out for but feeling as I do I fear it was for too long.

I reached the dining area and saw my father sitting there, patiently waiting for me. The boy was also sitting there talking to him until he noticed me. I walked in and sat at my seat across from my father. A plate was then presented in front of me, but instead of the usual disgusting meat pies, there was fruit and bread. I started to dig into the food.

"That was pretty silly of you, you know you could have died."

"It was a risk, I admit, but I wasn't going to let anyone be a casualty of your games." I turned my gaze to him, but he just returned it with a smile.

"Well as long as you're aware." He started to eat his food, but then he noticed my gaze turned toward the boy. "This is Sai, yes he is the same curse you re-birthed."

"Why is he here? Don't you usually take care of them?

"He is your responsibility, and he's been keeping me company since you decided to sleep for so long."

"And how long is, so long."

"You know how things are different down here, you will just have to wait until you return to find out."

"So, I can leave?"

"Of course."

He was being very passive, possibly too passive. "How did I get here?"

"I brought you here of course. You passed out in *his* arms. I told him the only way you would survive is if you came home to rest, so he passed you over, and voila here you are, alive."

He wasn't wrong, my Shadow self would heal faster keeping me alive until my magic was able to revive, making me stable again; but how long did this take?

"I'll leave after I'm done."

"Can't even spend one day with me?" He was being quite dramatic.

"I fear I have already missed enough time. I have to return." I looked at Sai, before returning my attention to my father. "You will just have to take care of him for a little longer."

"If you insist."

"What is going on here? You're not fighting about me leaving, and now you're going to do what I ask? What's your game?" I stood so fast my chair fell behind me.

"No game," He smiled, "I promise, I am just doing what I promised."

"And what did you promise?"

"Ah, that I do not have to say. It would be between me and your King, Master, lover, whatever it is he is to you."

"Fine! At least tell me why you gave Morgan such a powerful curse."

"My dear, what makes you think I did it?"

"I hunted for your curses until I could not feel or find anymore. Either you created him brand new or I missed it."

He smiled, "Ah, well it would be the latter in that little spiel of yours. You know I don't make those anymore. Someone found him, and handed him over to that woman."

"That would mean a very powerful witch would have had to find him to be able to just hand him over to be used by a mediocre vampire. Or they were still in control of it while she had him."

"Seems like you have a running theory though sadly I can not help you, my dear, you're the only witch I know of that could make a contract with Sai."

"Seems I better get to the surface faster than I thought. Goodbye father, please don't visit again." I left hopefully to never see him again, doubtful; but whoever this witch was I would have to find them. Who knows what else they were planning.

It didn't take me long to get back to my room. I threw my cloak back on before heading to the door. He made a pact with Gerard that I am certain, and I'll just have to beat some sense into him for thinking that was a good idea.

Once I reached the door they opened without any issues. Once I reached the other side of the bridge I moved to the surface. In a few seconds, I was standing on green grass under a blue sky with white fluffy clouds. It was warm on my face. I took a deep breath in, smelling the summer air. It was just Spring when I left, so a few months wasn't too bad.

Gerard' manor was just ahead, and I walked up the path towards it. Everything seemed the same, there were guards that were at their post. Once they spotted me, they looked surprised, but they didn't move.

Someone was coming out of the front entrance. At first, he looked like Gerard but then it was easy to tell he was not, he was too slim to be him. Once he stopped and his eyes fell into mine, I knew who it was.

"Angelic!" He sprinted to me, reaching me in a blink, engulfing me in a hug.

"Galen!" I was able to get out, even though I was being crushed.

He pushed back, giving me some space to breathe. "When did you get here?"

"Just now, I was just walking up the path."

"I haven't been around, so I thought..."

"Angelic!" We both turned to see a girl running towards us. She was petite with long light brown hair. It was Lucia, and by the length of her hair made me worry I was gone far longer than a couple of months could have grown.

She crashed into me, forcing me to try and keep us both upright. Her hug wasn't as tight as it usually was, and that's when I noticed a pronounced belly.

"Lucia, are you pregnant?"

She pulled back "I am!" She was smiling. "I saw you from the window. We were having a quick meeting."

"We?"

"Oh, well you see..."

I saw Eric and Gerard walk out of the entrance. Now I see, I smiled back at her. "I guess I should have seen that one coming." She was grinning from ear to ear. She was happy and that made me happy. "Lucia, how long has it been?"

"Three years." I heard Gerard' words. They hit me like lightning, that couldn't be possible.

"That can't be true." I stumbled backwards, trying to take in the enormity of the news. "I should be dead if that's the case."

"He promised to keep you alive."

"And what was the deal you had to make for it?"

He just smiled a bit, "I'm sure you have a lot of questions and are curious about a lot of things, come inside and we will try to answer as many as we can."

He turned and started heading inside. Lucia wrapped her arm around mine, and Galen put his arm over my shoulder. I'm sure whatever has happened won't be anything as shocking as what I just pulled off. The enormity of power should have killed me, but I lived. Maybe, someday, I could overpower my father.

SNEAK PEAK

"It's been years and we have had no leads!" Gerard fist smashed down on the Shadow Kings table. A little irritating but nothing The Shadow King wouldn't have expected.

"Calm down, this is nothing but expected. My daughter, let alone reckless and stubborn, has proven she can handle extraordinary power and live. Right now, the focus is on him so don't take it out on my table."

Gerard moved back, worried if he smashed anything else of the Shadow Kings, he would get a little bit more than just a warning.

"Now tell me what you know." The Shadow King ordered.

"Nothing, that's the problem. We're no closer to solving this issue than when we started three years ago."

"Ah, yes, well at least there is some good news, she will wake soon, and in that time, I will come to your table and give you a bit of advice."

Gerard didn't know what to take from this information. Was it a threat, a promise, or another deal?

"What about our first deal?"

"Well, that did keep my daughter alive, didn't it, and you

played your part perfectly, she wouldn't have noticed, that I can guarantee you."

It hurt Gerard knowing the first thing she woke up to would be a lie. If only he could break his promise but that would only put her in more danger.

The Shadow King moved in front of Gerard, "Now is the time to prepare. She will wake soon and when she does, she will know that someone else is playing the cards, and this person I know plans to destroy everything."

Gerard narrowed his eyes, "How can you be certain?"

"Why? Because they think as I do. Why not use the most unpredictable King to use as a tool towards war and see what the strengths of the other kings have that they can use against him." The Shadow King shrugged his shoulders before sitting and continued drinking his drink.

It irritated Gerard how he couldn't see the double edged sword that had been right in front of him. The moment Angelic passed out in the field; he knew that this was all a ploy. He wouldn't let this happen again, who knows how long she would be out next time, or maybe even survive.

"Just tell me when she wakes." Gerard started to walk out the doors.

"Oh, I won't," Gerard turned back with a curious look, "You really think the first thing she is going to do is stay with her dear ol dad?" The Shadow King got up and walked up to Gerard until he stood in front of him. "She will go back to you, and that night when you're all sitting and eating, trying to catch up on your lives and what she missed, I will join you, and tell her everything." He smiled at Gerard knowing this made him uncomfortable.

Gerard only replied, "See you at dinner." Before he turned and left.

Stirring in the distance a girl was waking up from her long slumber. It wasn't a night's rest that woke her but a nightmare